"Your adm⸻ ⸻r wallets ou⸻ ⸻ snorted

"This is a singles club, isn't it? Don't people usually buy drinks for each other?" Claire asked.

She had a point, but Mitch wasn't about to concede. Not when she'd started a brawl within half an hour of her arrival. Not when her antics threatened to distract him from his investigation. Not when he had an almost irresistible urge to kiss her sassy mouth.

Battling his libido, Mitch carried Claire out to the curb and hailed down a cab. Then he loosened his grip, allowing her to slide the rest of the way down his body. *Sweet torture.*

"Enjoying yourself?" she challenged.

"I like it better when you don't talk," he said, his body throbbing.

She narrowed her eyes. "Just try to stop me."

So he did. Lowering his head, he captured her sassy mouth with his own, figuring she'd pull back at any moment. Only she didn't.

What the hell was wrong with him? With her?

Stepping back, Mitch managed to hustle her into the cab before he lost total control. But he had the feeling that the fun was just starting....

Dear Reader,

Have you ever taken on a new challenge knowing you were in way over your head? This happens to me more times than I'd like to admit, so it seemed only natural to put my heroine in a similar predicament.

Professor Claire Dellafield is a small-town girl determined to study the power of love in the Big Apple. If only tough guy Mitch Malone would stop standing in her way! But with a little help from a special skirt and a spoiled poodle, Claire makes herself *Sheerly Irresistible,* and Mitch soon finds himself completely under her spell....

Sheerly Irresistible is the second book in the SINGLE IN THE CITY miniseries, caught right between Heather MacAllister's *Skirting the Issue* (August 2002) and Cara Summers's *Short, Sweet and Sexy* (October 2002). Don't miss any of the fun!

Happy reading,

Kristin Gabriel

P.S. I love to hear from readers. You can contact me through my Web site at www. KristinGabriel.com.

Books by Kristin Gabriel

HARLEQUIN TEMPTATION
834—DANGEROUSLY IRRESISTIBLE
868—SEDUCED IN SEATTLE

HARLEQUIN DUETS
 7—ANNIE, GET YOUR GROOM
25—THE BACHELOR TRAP
27—BACHELOR BY DESIGN
29—BEAUTY AND THE BACHELOR
61—OPERATION BABE-MAGNET
 —OPERATION BEAUTY

Kristin Gabriel
SHEERLY IRRESISTIBLE

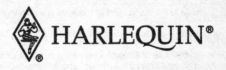

HARLEQUIN®

TORONTO • NEW YORK • LONDON
AMSTERDAM • PARIS • SYDNEY • HAMBURG
STOCKHOLM • ATHENS • TOKYO • MILAN • MADRID
PRAGUE • WARSAW • BUDAPEST • AUCKLAND

For Heather MacAllister and Cara Summers.
Thanks for making this book so much fun to write!

ISBN 0-373-25996-4

SHEERLY IRRESISTIBLE

1

"THAT'S IT," THE photographer said, looking at her through the camera lens. "Arch your back. There... now pout for me. Think sultry."

Unfortunately, Claire Dellafield couldn't think about anything except how ridiculous it was for a cultural anthropologist to be draped across a Dumpster in a back alley in New York City. This was definitely not what she'd imagined doing on her first day in the most exciting city in the world.

Unpeeling herself from the garbage bin, she plucked the collar of the tank top away from her damp cleavage. "Look, I assumed we were just going to take a few simple headshots in front of the nightclub. A publicity photo the university could send out when they release the results of my research project. This," she motioned to the narrow back alley, "just doesn't make sense."

The photographer lowered his camera. "I am Evan Wang. I take direction from no one. You are the model. I'm the artist. You must trust me."

"I'm not a model," she clarified, just to make certain Evan hadn't confused his assignments. "I'm an anthropology professor."

"Yes, that is a problem," Evan mused, studying her from a different angle. "But that's why people call me the miracle worker."

Claire swallowed a groan, wishing she'd followed her instincts and turned down this research project. But that simply wasn't a luxury a rookie anthropologist could afford. Not when research grants were so few and far between. So she'd reluctantly agreed when Penleigh College approached her to revisit a study called *Strangers in the Night* that had made both her father and the college famous twenty-five years ago. No doubt, some would continue to accuse her of riding her father's coattails.

Sometimes she wondered if they were right.

Claire lifted her long, thick hair off the back of her neck, hoping a cool breeze would find its way into the alley. It had never been this hot in Penleigh, Indiana, the small college town she'd called home her entire life. She had shared a cottage with her father on campus until nine months ago, when he'd passed away after a long battle with kidney disease. Then it seemed as if she'd just stepped into his life—taking over his classes and now, reprising his famous research project.

Thinking of her father made Claire's throat tighten. Marcus Dellafield had been in this same spot twenty-five years ago. Well, maybe not this *exact* spot. There had been no sexy pictures to accompany his study on human mating habits at The Jungle, once the most popular singles bar in New York City.

But Professor Dellafield had done more than just collected research all those years ago. He'd adopted Claire as an infant and brought her back with him to Penleigh, raising her as a single father. That's what had captured the media's attention—the story of an ivory tower professor who gave a child born out of wedlock a fairy-tale life.

And it *had* been like a fairy tale. Claire's father had taken her with him on all his anthropological research trips, showing her the world in the process. She'd been to places like Borneo and Tasmania. Eaten with the Maori of New Zealand. Traveled by riverboat on the Amazon in South America.

And she'd enjoyed every moment of it. So had her father. During the last months of his illness, he'd often told her that he had no regrets. Nothing had been left undone. He'd always lived his life to the very fullest.

Claire planned to do the same. Only life didn't always cooperate with her. Maybe once she completed this research project, she could begin to live her own dreams, make her own choices.

"I've got an idea," Evan said at last. "Let's take advantage of your natural innocence. We'll go for the Mary Richards look."

"Mary Richards?" Claire echoed in confusion.

"You know," Evan said, digging into his big, yellow satchel, "from the old *Mary Tyler Moore Show*. A single girl in the city, ready to turn the world on with her smile."

"I know who she is," Claire replied. Unlike most

parents, her father had actively encouraged her to watch as many movies and television shows as possible. He believed they were a reflection of the changing mores of modern culture—especially the sitcom reruns—and worthy of study.

"Here we go," Evan exclaimed, pulling a raspberry pink beret out of the satchel. He brushed off the lint, then handed it to her. "Put it on."

She placed the beret on her head. "How's that?"

"Perfect! I can almost hear the theme song to the show." He adjusted the brim, then stepped back and framed her between his fingers. "Now lose the blouse."

She looked down at her yellow cotton blouse, then shrugged and took it off, leaving only the white tank top underneath to go with her khaki shorts.

"Much better," Evan said, looping the camera strap over his neck. "Now stand up and lean against the door. Pretend it's a man and make love to it."

Claire rose to her feet, frowning at the tattered screen door streaked with rust. "I don't remember Mary making love to any doors."

He heaved a tortured sigh. "It's all we have at the moment. Just work with me here."

The screen door suddenly opened, catching Claire in the shin. "Ow!"

"Excuse me," muttered a man backing out of the door. He was tall, dark and shirtless.

He turned to face her, a crate of empty beer bottles in his arms. But it was the sight of his bare, broad chest that had Claire's mouth watering. Along with the raven hair slicked back off his forehead, the shadow of whiskers on his square jaw, and his startling blue eyes. She swallowed hard to keep from drooling.

The man raised his voice, laced now with impatience. "Excuse me."

She stumbled off the step to let him pass and he set the crate of beer bottles next to a recycling bin, then disappeared inside the nightclub once more.

"Sir," Evan shouted after him, bounding up the back step. The man appeared at the door a moment later carrying another crate of empty bottles.

"Can you help us out here?" Evan asked.

"What do you need?"

"My name is Evan and this is Mary," he said, motioning to her.

"Claire," she corrected.

"Whatever," Evan replied with a dismissive wave of his hand. "And you are?"

The man hesitated a moment, taking stock of them both. "Mitch Malone."

"Well, Mitch, I'm trying to finish up a photo shoot and Mary here, I mean Claire, is having trouble making love to the door. I thought if she had a human prop it might work better."

Mitch didn't even blink at the odd request. "Sorry, but I have twenty more crates to haul out here."

"Perfect. That's just what we need." Evan reached

out and positioned Claire in front of him. "You find him attractive, don't you?"

She cleared her throat as Mitch's gaze moved to her face. He had the bluest eyes she'd ever seen. "I'm...I mean...he seems very nice."

"Mitch is more than nice." Evan told her, grabbing his camera once more. "He's everything you've ever desired in a man. Now show me how much you want him. Try to seduce him with some great body language as he moves in and out of the building."

Claire turned to Evan as a hot flush crept into her cheeks. "Is this *really* necessary?"

Evan held up both hands. "No questions, remember? I am the artist here."

"I'm going back to work now," Mitch said, setting down the crate.

"Yes, go right ahead." Evan began snapping a rapid succession of pictures as Mitch walked back inside the building. "Okay, now wait for him, Claire...there he is...now remember, we want hot. We want sultry."

Claire sidled out of Mitch's way as he deposited another crate on the ground, feeling more ridiculous by the minute. It didn't help matters that he seemed totally oblivious to her. She tried sultry. She tried pouting. She even tried opening the door for him and striking a sexy pose against it, but she only succeeded in popping out the screen.

"Keep going. We're getting there," Evan told her, snapping a few more pictures as she just stood there with her hands on her hips while Mitch strode past her once more.

It didn't help matters that she couldn't seem to take her eyes off him. Of course, the man was only half-dressed. A light sheen of perspiration glowed on his tanned skin, his powerful muscles flexing in his thick chest and broad shoulders.

She'd seen scantily clad men before on her travels, but there was something mesmerizing about the way this man's body moved. He had an easy grace that made most of the men at Penleigh, in their tweed jackets and loafers, seem stuffy by comparison. Mitch was definitely a product of his environment. Solid. Earthy. Primal.

Somehow he made the alley seem even hotter than before.

"Not bad," Evan said at last, popping another roll of film into his camera. "Now let's try some Mary poses. We're going for the carefree look. Try tossing the beret into the air."

She stepped away from the back entrance of The Jungle, more than ready to finish this photo shoot. "Like this?" She threw the beret high into the air, squinting against the bright June sun.

"Good," Evan said as the camera whirred. "Now do it again. But I want you to catch it this time."

Claire picked up the beret, hearing the screen door squeak once again. Out of the corner of her eye, she saw Mitch set another crate on the ground. Determined to show him the same amount of indifference he was showing her, she tossed the beret high into the air. Only her throw was a little off and she had to walk backward as it fluttered toward the ground. She skidded on a crushed tin can, lost her balance, and landed against something hard and warm.

Mitch.

He braced his large hands on her hips to steady her. "You okay?"

She gulped in a deep breath, well aware of his long fingers spanning her waist. Her back was against his bare chest and she inhaled a musky aroma that was all male. "I'm fine."

He let go of her, then bent down to pick up the beret. "Here you go, Mary."

"Claire," she breathed through dry lips.

"Whatever."

2

An hour later, Claire forced both the photo shoot and Mitch Malone completely out of her mind. Excitement fluttered in her chest as she climbed out of a taxi at Central Park West, then waited while the driver retrieved her bags from the trunk. The Willoughby towered in front of her, a high-rise apartment building with art deco trim on the facade.

Her godmother, Petra Gerard, lived here and Claire couldn't wait to see her again. But first she had to get past the young man who sat sprawled on a lawn chair inside the glass-enclosed foyer of the building. He wore baggy blue polka dot swimming trunks, mirrored sunglasses, and green-tinted zinc oxide on his narrow aquiline nose.

As she dragged her suitcases through the heavy plate glass door, he didn't even look up. Just sat there humming to the music emanating from the boom box, his skinny feet soaking in a blue plastic wading pool.

She paused to catch her breath as the Beach Boys began singing about "California Girls."

"If you don't give me the password," the man said, his head propped on the lawn chair with a rolled-up orange beach towel. "I will be forced to stop you with the Venetian death grip."

"And you are?" Her gaze fell on his pale, hairless chest. Then she noticed the tattoo on his upper left bicep. It looked like a small schnauzer.

"I'm Franco Rossi. Aspiring actor, black belt in karate and judo, and temporary doorman." He slid his sunglasses up on top of his head, then followed her gaze to his arm. "It's Toto. The tattoo, not the password. I happen to be a big fan of *The Wizard Of Oz*."

"Oh," she said, wondering if he was mentally stable.

He smiled, "You're not in Kansas anymore."

"I'm from Indiana."

"Same difference."

Claire set both her suitcases on the polished marble floor. "I'm here to see Petra Gerard. She's expecting me."

"Ah, Petra." Franco smiled. "She's one of my favorite tenants. A little absentminded, though."

That was putting it mildly. Petra always blamed her total inattention to detail on her muse. A former art professor at Penleigh, Claire's godmother had been one of Marcus Dellafield's best friends and a frequent visitor to their home. Bubbly and a little eccentric, Petra had more energy than many women half her age. She'd retired from teaching at sixty and moved to Manhattan, embarking on a very lucrative second career as a sculptress.

"Could you please let her know I'm here. My name is Claire Dellafield."

"Love to, Claire," Franco purred, "if you can front me the airfare to Bermuda. Petra left a week ago and I'm not sure when she's coming back."

Claire's heart sunk to her toes. "Bermuda?"

He swished his toes in the pool water. "She's competing in the senior division of the Ms. Universe fitness pageant. Knowing Petra, she'll probably come home with the title."

Claire shook her head. "Petra can't be in Bermuda. She's supposed to introduce me to a Mr. McLain. I'm subletting his apartment for the summer."

He sighed. "You and everyone else in this city. There's already a crowd up there waiting for the auction."

"Auction?"

"Petra should have filled you in on all the juicy details, but she probably believed Tavish when he promised not to do it anymore." Franco leaned forward and lowered his voice to a furtive whisper, even though they were alone in the foyer. "Tavish McLain auctions off his place every summer. Last year a blond ballerina and a Madonna clone battled over it. The ballerina even offered an incentive package, if you know what I mean. Tavish has a thing for blondes, so he enjoyed every minute of it."

Claire leaned against the plate glass door, vaguely aware that the faint odor of the Dumpster still clung to her clothes. With Petra out of the country, she didn't have anywhere else to go and certainly not enough money to spend the summer in a New York City hotel room. She wondered if camping in Central Park would be any more dangerous than pitching a tent on the African savannah.

Franco waved her away. "You're blocking my sun. I'm trying to get a tan here."

Then he groaned as another woman walked purposefully toward the building. "Here comes another one. How am I supposed to relax with people streaming in and out of here all day?"

Claire glanced at the woman who entered the foyer. She looked nice. And blond. Just McLain's type—unless Claire got to him first. She turned back to Franco. "I need to see Tavish McLain. Immediately."

"Password!"

"Can you give me a hint?"

"I'm waaaaaiiiiting," Franco crooned.

"Toto," the blonde ventured, her gaze on Franco's arm.

"Close but no cigar." Then he burst into the opening stanza of "Somewhere Over the Rainbow," before collecting himself. "Are you here for the apartment?"

"Yes," they replied simultaneously.

"This is McLain's day of glory," Franco declared. "The day he lives the other three hundred and sixty-four days of the year dreaming of. He is surrounded by women."

"We'd like to join them," the blonde said.

Franco leaned closer to them and whispered, "You

might try naming the actor who played the cowardly lion."

Claire exchanged glances with the blonde, then they both blurted, "Bert Lahr."

"Excellent," Franco replied with a grin.

"Bert Lahr is the password, then?" the blonde asked.

"No. But I like the fact that you're both *Wizard of Oz* movie buffs, so you may pass."

Claire turned back to Franco as the blonde pressed the elevator button. "Now how about giving me a hint to win over McLain?"

Franco shrugged. "Like I said, he's into blondes. But maybe you could show a little cleavage, wiggle your hips and see what happens."

Claire glanced down at her tank top. Mitch Malone hadn't seemed too impressed with her cleavage. Not that she should care about the opinion of a total stranger. A street-smart tough who probably treated women like toys. Definitely not her type.

Not by a long shot.

A loud ding announced the elevator's arrival, breaking her reverie. She grabbed her suitcases and headed for the elevator, the blonde helping her heave the biggest one inside.

"Thanks," Claire said, as the doors slid closed. "I'm Claire Dellafield."

"A. J. Potter," the blonde replied with an assessing glance. "I guess we're competitors."

She sighed. "I don't have enough money to be much competition."

"Want to join forces and bid together?"

Live with a complete stranger? "I don't know. I..."

"Smart girl. Someone warned you about the big, bad city." A.J. reached into her purse. "I just heard that the bidding might be brutal and I intend to win. Think about it."

The elevator doors opened on the sixth floor and Claire dragged her suitcases into the crowded hallway. There were two other apartments on the floor, but it was obvious which one belonged to McLain. Dozens of people jammed around the open doorway.

"I think it's going to take more than cleavage," Claire muttered to herself. A dog growled and she turned to see a poodle in the arms of a woman wearing a pink caftan and matching pink bouffant hair.

"Hush, Cleo," the older woman crooned to the dog. "That mean Mr. McLain is going away soon. Then you'll have somebody new to take you on walksies."

Claire and A.J. squeezed their way into the apartment just in time to hear the bidding war start. There were blondes in all shapes and sizes. Claire sank down on her big suitcase, wondering how could she possibly compete.

"This is ridiculous," A.J. muttered, then whipped out her cell phone.

Claire looked up to see a tall brunette approaching them. At least she wasn't the only nonblonde here.

The brunette glanced at A.J., then turned her attention back to Claire. "This is really something, isn't it?"

"Not exactly what I expected." She motioned to the suitcases. "I was planning to move in here today. Now I don't know what I'm going to do."

The brunette shifted the package she held from one arm to the other. "This is your lucky day. I work for a hotel. Therefore, I can promise you won't sleep on the street tonight. And you can treat yourself to a nice, hot bubble bath."

Yikes. Maybe Claire wasn't the only one who could smell the Dumpster on her clothes. But she wasn't quite ready to declare herself a charity case yet. "I can't—"

"Oh, I got that part," the brunette said, lowering her voice. "You'd be in one of the unrentable rooms. No charge."

This woman was trying to change the reputation of uncaring New Yorkers in one fell swoop. "Why would you do that? You don't even know me."

"Because I can. Because helping the sisterhood was something my mother drilled into me. And, hey, I get off on warm, fuzzy feelings in my tummy."

A.J. laughed. "So do I, but they don't come from giving away freebie hotel rooms."

The brunette grinned at her. "Samantha Baldwin."

"A. J. Potter." The two women shook hands. "You sounded like a madam gathering the poor waif into her house of ill repute. I think you scared her."

"I'm not scared," Claire said, "just fascinated by

abnormal human behavior. Abnormal for a New Yorker, anyway."

She thought of Mitch's behavior this afternoon and a flush of heat washed up her neck. Could the man have been any more oblivious to her? No one had ever called her a beauty, but men hadn't run screaming from her, either. She was average weight and height, taller than A.J., but shorter than Samantha. She'd been tempted to highlight her long brown hair, but simply hadn't found the time after taking over her father's class schedule. Her unusual topaz brown eyes were her best feature and she often wondered if she'd inherited them from the mother who had given her up for adoption. She glanced down at the emerald ring on her right hand, the vibrant color reminding her of her father's eyes. He'd given her the ring on her sixteenth birthday. They'd been on a research trip in South America that summer and she'd had a crush on one of his graduate students, but the man had been oblivious to her.

A disturbing trend.

For the first time, she wondered if there was something wrong with her. She hadn't dated much at Penleigh, but she'd assumed that was because most of the men on campus knew about her father's illness.

What if there was another reason? Claire mentally shook herself, realizing now wasn't the time to obsess about her love life, or lack of one. She needed to focus on this research project and try to find some way to bring a fresh twist to the subject of dating. *Strangers in the Night* had been one of the first of its kind to study the effect of the sexual revolution on young singles. So many similar studies had followed that Claire couldn't imagine finding anything new to add to the field. Something she tried to communicate to the board of directors at Penleigh, but they hadn't wanted to listen.

Which just made it all the harder to prove herself in the anthropology world, though not impossible. But first she had to find a place to stay.

Maybe she should accept Samantha's offer of the free hotel room, then move in with Petra when she returned from Bermuda. Unfortunately, Claire had no idea when that might be. Knowing Petra, it could be next week or next year.

"What's your name?"

Claire blinked, then noticed both women looking at her. She'd completely lost track of the conversation. "Claire Dellafield. Why?"

Samantha gestured to her. "Get with the program. We're forming a rental coalition. You want in?"

Claire rose off her suitcase, sensing her luck was about to change. "You mean we'd room together?"

"Mental functions appear to be intact," A.J. said. "You smoke?"

Claire shook her head. "But I can learn."

Samantha laughed. "She's in for the entertainment value alone."

Claire looked at both of them, realizing it would be the first time in her life she'd ever lived with women close to her own age. As much as she'd loved her father, she couldn't help but feel that sometimes her life had been laid out like a map, with all the routes already chosen for her. Now she was charting new territory. It was both thrilling and terrifying.

"How much can you contribute to rent?" A.J. asked.

Claire did a quick calculation of her bank account. "Eight hundred."

"That's forty-six hundred," A.J. exhaled. "Surely the rent won't go as high as that."

The door opened and the crowd turned in unison to see two men walk into the room.

Several people cried out a name. "Tavish!"

"Let's play this out," A.J. advised under her breath.

Claire noticed several of the blondes adjusting their blouses as Tavish moved to the center of the room. He reminded her of a medicine man she'd seen once in Central America. He'd worn a putrid green robe, almost the same shade as Tavish McLain's faux leather vest. They both shared the same cocky walk, too. As if they believed they controlled the universe. Or at least their own small portion of it.

"Stand in front of me," Samantha ordered, suddenly reaching around her back to unzip her skirt.

Claire watched in disbelief as the woman shimmied her skirt down her legs. "What are you doing?"

"I think I may have something that will persuade Mr. McLain to give us anything we want."

"What?" A.J. asked. "A gun?"

"Even better," Samantha replied, unwrapping the package in her arms, then pulling out a wad of silky black fabric. "A magic skirt."

Claire and A.J. exchanged skeptical glances. Then Claire cleared her throat. "Did you say a *magic* skirt?"

"I know it sounds crazy." Samantha shook out the wrinkles. "But it's a man-magnet. The skirt apparently originated from the Caribbean, where there's a special fibrous root that the native women spin into a thread. That thread runs through this skirt. Men will do anything for the woman who wears it."

"You're kidding," A.J. said, looking like Claire felt. Maybe Samantha wasn't such a great choice for a roommate after all. Unless you were a mental patient at Bellevue. Samantha pulled on the black skirt. "Look, I don't believe it, either, but it can't hurt." She handed her jacket to Claire, then smoothed the black skirt over her thighs.

Claire had to admit it looked nice. The fabric had a very unusual sheen, but she certainly didn't see anything magical about it.

"Follow me, ladies," Samantha said, then moved toward Tavish.

A.J. looked at Claire, then shrugged. "What can it hurt?"

"True," Claire replied, as they walked behind Sam. "And if it doesn't work, we can always resort to Plan B."

"What's Plan B?" A.J. asked.

"We hang Tavish out his window by the ankles until he agrees to sublet us his apartment."

A.J. smiled. "So it's a win-win situation. If we drop him, another vacancy opens up."

But amazingly enough, the skirt did work. Claire watched in sheer disbelief as Tavish's jaw sagged when he caught sight of Samantha. His gaze became slightly unfocused and he stared unblinking at the skirt. It was as if he'd been drugged.

The next thing she knew, A.J. was handing over a check for two thousand dollars.

Tavish smiled. "So you want to pay all the rent up front?" He stuck the check in his vest pocket. "The perfect tenant, wouldn't you say, Roger?"

"I'd say so." The broker sidled closer to Samantha.

Something didn't add up. "But wait," Claire interjected. "I thought that was just for..." A warning pinch on her arm cut her off in midsentence. "Ow!"

"That should be tenants." Samantha motined to A.J. and Claire. "My roommates."

Claire smiled tightly at the man as she rubbed her sore arm. There was no mistake. Tavish was giving them his apartment for the entire summer. For only two thousand dollars. Claire glanced down at the skirt Samantha wore, no longer a skeptic.

While A.J. and Sam finalized the deal with the broker, Claire helped herd the disappointed bidders out of the apartment before Tavish had a chance to change his mind. Then she returned to the circle with her new roommates, Tavish and the broker just in time to hear the tail end of the conversation.

"Cleo's the poodle," the broker said. "Lives in 6B. You'll have to walk her. It's part of Tavish's arrangement with his neighbors."

"No problem," A.J. said, quickly scribbling her signature beneath Samantha's, then handing the pen to Claire.

"I can't believe you did it!" A.J. exclaimed to Sam after everyone had left. Then all three of them began to high-five each other.

"That skirt did it," Claire murmured to herself, enthralled by what she'd just seen. She'd traveled enough with her father to know several cultures believed certain objects and plants had aphrodisiac powers, but she'd never witnessed an actual demonstration before.

She made a mental note to research the skirt on the Internet tonight. Perhaps she could find the country of origin. Then another thought hit her. What if she did her next research project on aphrodisiacs and their effect on different cultures around the world? A study she could call all her own.

But no university would give her a grant if she failed in her current research project. Forming a good rapport with potential subjects at The Jungle would be crucial to that success.

If Samantha let her borrow that skirt...

Claire's skin prickled at the possibilities. If she could elicit even half the reaction she'd just seen in

Tavish, finding volunteers to take part in her research project wouldn't be any problem. And she could use the opportunity to study the skirt's effect at the same time. Especially on a man like Mitch Malone, who had been totally oblivious to her only a few hours ago.

Maybe she could turn the world on with her smile after all.

3

THE NEXT DAY, MITCH STOOD outside St. Luke's hospital, wondering if he should have listened to his grandmother and entered the priesthood instead of pursuing a career as a cop. She'd worried about the dangers of police work, but Mitch had never suffered more than a few bumps and bruises on the job.

He only wished he could say the same of his partner, Elaine O'Brien.

Mitch had found excuse after excuse to avoid visiting Elaine since she'd been brought here by ambulance a week ago. He'd called almost every day, but he couldn't stand the thought of seeing his partner confined to a hospital bed.

Because of him.

Mitch had replayed that terrible morning over and over in his mind. They were supposed to meet an anonymous informant who promised to give them a lead in the Vandalay case. Dick Vandalay, owner of The Jungle nightclub, was suspected of trafficking in illegal substances. Specifically, bootleg Viagra and various imported animal parts, like rhinoceros horns, that were purported to increase a man's sexual prowess.

The Jungle had been struggling to stay in business, with singles' bars becoming passé in this age of personal ads and Internet dating sites. So Vandalay definitely had motivation to cater to customers who were desperate for love. As well as the opportunity.

What the police lacked was hard evidence. They knew the stuff was flowing out of the nightclub, they just didn't know how it was coming in. Vandalay's record was squeaky clean, but he was still the most likely suspect. His family tree read like a *Who's Who* of drug dealers and other assorted felons. Now they just needed to find the right limb to hang him from.

The informant had promised to do just that, the morning of June first. But Mitch had been late, thanks to a woman he'd met the night before. He rubbed one hand over his jaw, still unable to believe she'd turned off the alarm without waking him.

Elaine had finally given up on Mitch and gone on to meet the informant by herself. Only the informant must have panicked, because when Mitch finally arrived at the abandoned building that had been preselected as their meeting place, he'd found Elaine at the bottom of a staircase with a concussion and a shattered hip.

Now she was in this place, recovering from the hip injury that might keep her off the vice squad and tied to a police desk for the rest of her career. But Elaine didn't know that yet and Mitch wasn't about to tell her. She loved investigative work too much to give it up. That's why she'd practically set up a command post from her bed, calling him with all the background information she'd gathered and any possible leads on the case.

Maybe she sensed it would be her last one.

He took a deep breath, realizing he'd been a coward long enough. Then he walked through the automatic doors of the hospital and into a booby trap—also known as the gift shop. He didn't want to come into his partner's room empty-handed, but his gift-giving record was pretty bleak. It had started when he was fifteen, the time he'd given his first girlfriend a pet rat for Valentine's Day. She'd screamed, dropped the rat, and her parents had been forced to call an exterminator to catch it. Then they'd sent his grandmother the bill.

The first of many disasters.

Mitch turned in a slow circle around the gift shop, waiting for something to call out to him. A set of ceramic clowns? A jigsaw puzzle? A book of brain teasers?

"May I help you?"

He looked down to see a tiny silver-haired lady standing in front of him. She wore a salmon-pink frock and a pair of bifocals.

"I'm looking for a gift for a colleague of mine."

"Male or female?" the woman asked with a toothy smile.

"Female."

She motioned to the counter behind her. "We have some lovely potpourri."

"You mean those bags of dead flowers?"

"They're very fragrant," she said, handing one to him. "This one is called Spring Blossom."

He held it up to his nose. "Nice. But what are you supposed to do with it?"

"You can place potpourri in a bowl or other decorative container to give the room a nice, fresh scent."

He scowled down at the price tag. Twenty bucks for stuff he could rake up in his backyard? "I don't think this is what I'm looking for."

"Well, we have some nice jewelry." She pointed to another shelf. "Perhaps a bracelet?"

His last girlfriend had hated those glow-in-the-dark earrings he'd given her. Then his gaze fell on a small box shoved toward the back of the top shelf and he knew he'd found the perfect gift.

Mitch pointed up to it. "That's what I want."

The clerk stood up on her tiptoes, then her forehead crinkled. "Are you sure?"

He grinned, already imagining the expression on Elaine's face. "Positive."

Ten minutes later, he stood outside the door to her room, the gift bag in his hand and a sick feeling in the pit of his stomach. He hated the smell of hospitals. Maybe he should have bought her that potpourri after all. Mitch half turned, ready to head back to the gift shop, but he knew he was just delaying the inevitable. Raising his fist, he rapped on the door.

"Come in."

He pushed the door open and saw Elaine seated in

a chair by the window, wearing bulky gray sweat-pants and a Yankees T-shirt. She was ten years his senior, but the freckles on her cheeks made her appear younger. Her ash-blond hair was pulled back in a ponytail and she looked thinner than she had a week ago. He forced his stiff lips into a smile.

Her green eyes lit up when she saw him standing in the doorway. "Hey, stranger!"

"You're out of bed."

"As much as possible. I make a lousy invalid."

"You look good." Then he awkwardly stuck out the gift bag in his hand. "I brought you something."

"Please let it be a six-pack of Moosehead," she implored, taking it from him.

"I didn't think you were supposed to drink in here."

She smiled. "Since when do you ever follow the rules, Malone?"

"Okay, I'll sneak in some beer on my next visit."

"Promise?" she asked, pushing the tissue paper aside and reaching into the gift bag.

"Promise," he replied, waiting to see her reaction.

She stared at the box for a long moment. "A beach ball."

"Inflatable. I thought it would be good exercise for you to bounce it around the room."

One corner of her mouth twitched. "Gee, Mitch, I...don't know what to say."

"Want me to blow it up for you?"

"Sure." She tossed him the box.

He removed the flattened plastic ball from inside, then flipped open the air valve and began to blow.

"So what's new on the case?"

He lifted his head. "I'm working undercover as a bouncer at The Jungle.

Her eyes widened. "I thought the captain nixed that idea when we proposed it three weeks ago."

"That was before you got hurt."

She nodded, understanding the intense emotions that surfaced when a fellow officer was injured in the line of duty. Their captain was now committed to solving this case, no matter how much manpower or how many resources it took.

So was Mitch. He'd even temporarily sworn off women—his penance for letting himself be distracted by a pretty face. Although his resolve had certainly been tested yesterday with that hot little number coming onto him in the back alley of The Jungle. He could still see that snug white tank top she wore, damp with perspiration, clinging to her chest in a way that left little to the imagination. But he'd passed the test and was determined to pay more attention to his job and less attention to his hormones until they closed this case.

"Earth to Mitch."

He blinked, then saw Elaine watching him. "Sorry."

"What's her name?"

He puffed a few more times into the beach ball. "Who?"

"The current dish on the Malone buffet."

"I'm not seeing anyone." He clamped his mouth on the rubber tube and blew until the ball was fully inflated. Then he pushed the cap in to seal it.

"How is that possible?" she teased. "Women have been falling at your feet since you took your first baby step. I'm married to a wonderful guy, so I'm immune to it, but I've seen the effect you have on the female population."

And she'd paid for it, thanks to that damn alarm clock. He tossed the beach ball to her. "I thought we were talking about the Vandalay case."

She caught the ball with both hands. "A case that's been going nowhere. But that might change now that you're working at The Jungle."

Mitch nodded. "All we need to do is identify Vandalay's supplier. Then we can nail the guy and bring the entire operation down."

He made it sound easy, but Mitch knew all too well how complex a drug ring could be. Growing up on the streets of New York, he'd met his first drug dealer when he was six, and been recruited as a courier a year later. His parents were two of the dealer's best customers. When they'd been arrested, he'd gone to live with his maternal grandmother. An arrangement that became permanent when his parents jumped bail.

They'd never come back.

Mitch assumed they were dead and he truly believed he might have been too if his grandmother hadn't stepped in and helped set his life straight.

"I'll keep working from it on this end," Elaine promised, breaking into his reverie. "It's that or go stir crazy in this place. I can't wait to get back out in the field."

He couldn't look at her. Not when he knew her career might never be the same again. It made him more determined than ever to bring Vandalay to justice. To do something, *anything*, to assuage this guilt roiling around inside of him.

"Hey." She bounced the beach ball off his forehead. "You keep drifting off on me."

He stood up. "Sorry. It's been a long week. One of the bartenders at The Jungle quit, so I've been pulling double shifts until Vandalay hires a replacement."

"The joys of undercover work." She reached for a file folder on the table beside her. "The other employees at the nightclub check out, by the way. No felony records. No connections with any criminal activity."

He nodded, then glanced at his watch. "I'd better take off. The Jungle opens in less than an hour."

She shifted on the chair, a spasm of pain crossing her face. "Okay. Keep me posted."

"Absolutely," he said, then waved to her before he walked out the door. Out in the hallway, he sucked in a deep breath of air. So far, this investigation was going nowhere. But Mitch refused to let his partner down again. He'd find a break in this case even if it killed him.

And if he had to resist the charms of another woman like the one in the tank top this afternoon, it just might.

TWO WEEKS AFTER HER arrival in New York City, Claire walked awkwardly into the living room of her apartment, teetering on the three-inch strapless black heels A.J. had lent her for the biggest night of her life. This was to be her first foray into The Jungle, on the hunt for volunteers for her research project.

"Wow," Sam observed from the sofa, "Franco was right. Rose really is your color."

Franco had done the girls' colors a few days ago, announcing that Claire was a soft autumn and must wear rose, turquoise and jade from now on.

Claire glanced down at the rose silk camisole she'd bought on a shopping spree with A.J. this afternoon. They'd also found black skirts at Bloomingdale's by a designer named Daryl that were identical to the one Sam owned. But Claire needed the real thing tonight, so she'd left her skirt in the closet and borrowed Sam's, along with a pair of gold hoop earrings.

"Am I missing anything?" Claire asked.

"Birth control?" A.J. quipped. "After all, you are conducting a study of human mating behavior."

"I will simply be an observer," Claire replied, "not an active participant."

"Speaking of mating behavior," Sam chimed, "Mrs. Higgenbotham brought over Cleo's appointment calendar so we can coordinate the walking schedule. Her poodle sees a therapist twice a week for canine intimacy dysfunction."

"She also has to appear in small claims court," A.J. added. "I'm representing her."

"Mrs. Higgenbotham?" Claire asked, adjusting the waistband of the skirt. The fabric was oddly warm to the touch.

"No, Cleo. Mrs. H has been trying to breed her, but it seems the poodle isn't interested in romance. When one of Cleo's suitors got too amorous, she bit him in a...sensitive place." A.J. grinned. "You might want to keep that strategy in mind, Claire, in case any of those men get too frisky with you tonight."

"I don't think that will be a problem," Claire said, grabbing her purse off the sofa. "Once I explain the reason I'm there."

Sam looked thoughtful. "Wouldn't your research be more effective if no one at the nightclub knew you were watching them?"

"It's not that kind of study," Claire explained. "I'll be recording general observations about The Jungle, as well as studying the dating habits of some of its regular patrons. I'll need to schedule in-depth interviews and ask questions about the average duration of relationships, the elements of physical, sociological and spiritual attraction, verbal and nonverbal interaction...things like that."

She saw Sam and A.J.'s eyes glaze over and a prickle of apprehension skittered down her spine.

Even Claire was bored by the subject. So how could she possibly succeed?

Then Sam blinked. "Oh, I almost forgot! I finally located Kate Gannon's e-mail address. It's on a sticky note by your computer."

"Who's Kate Gannon?" A.J. asked.

"She's the woman who owned the skirt before Sam." Claire looped the purse strap over her shoulder. "I want to find out more about its origin for my next research project." She took a deep breath. "But first I have to make it through this one."

"Knock 'em dead," A.J. said as Claire moved toward the door.

"And tell us all the juicy details when you get home," Sam called after her.

Claire just hoped there was something to tell. What if wearing the skirt had no effect on the men around her? What if they were all as oblivious to her as Mitch Malone had been? What if this research project was an abysmal failure?

Then the elevator doors opened on the main floor and Franco whistled at her.

"Be still my heart," he cried, clasping his hand to his chest. "Damn girl, you almost make me wish I was straight."

"So I look all right?" she asked, performing a slow twirl around the foyer.

"There's only one thing missing." Franco picked up a small shopping bag next to the door and handed it to her. "Here."

Claire pulled out a rose silk scarf. "It's beautiful."

"The perfect finishing touch," Franco replied, taking it from her and tying it in a jaunty knot around her neck. Then his gray eyes got misty. "I feel like Glinda the Good Witch, ready to send you off on the yellow brick road."

"I'll settle for a yellow taxi," she replied, leaning over to kiss his cheek. "Thanks, Franco."

"Off with you now, Dorothy." He pushed her out the door. "And watch out for those flying monkeys!"

MITCH SMELLED TROUBLE.

He stood at his post near the front entrance of The Jungle nightclub, his eyes slowly scanning the large room. The place was filling up fast tonight, with the men outnumbering the women two-to-one. White wicker ceiling fans stained to a dull brown from thirty years of smoke whirled overhead. The slight breeze they gave couldn't counteract the humid night air that blew inside every time the door opened.

Like most nightclubs, the lights in The Jungle were dimmed low enough to obscure facial features and the music was loud enough to prevent in-depth conversations. A few people danced on the wood parquet floor and the bartenders kept up a stream of steady business.

Mitch could sense the restlessness in the crowd tonight. Typical for a Friday, when everyone was ready to blow off steam after a long workweek. The man he'd been assigned to watch, Dick Vandalay, stood behind the bar training a new bartender. A young kid who looked like he might wet his pants if Vandalay yelled at him again.

A heated expletive shifted Mitch's attention to the dance floor, where a scuffle had just broken out. By the time he got there, the two women had each other by the hair. The man they were fighting over just stood off to the side with a drunken grin on his face.

"Break it up," Mitch said, pulling the women apart.

"Hey, keep out of this," the man said. "I was just starting to have some fun."

Both women lashed out at each other with skinny arms and bony fists. Mitch held them just far enough apart to keep them from doing any serious damage.

"If this is the kind of fun you want," Mitch told the man between clenched teeth, "then go somewhere else to have it."

The man took a step toward him. "Make me."

The unmistakable challenge in his tone made both women stop struggling and shift their focus to Mitch. He let go of them and faced the man on the dance floor. "If you're smart, you'll just turn around and walk away."

But Mitch knew there was little chance of that happening. This guy was like too many of the men he'd seen while living on the streets. Too macho to keep out of trouble until they were in it neck-deep. He glanced over at the bar and saw Vandalay nod.

Out of the corner of his eye, he glimpsed a beefy fist shooting out toward his jaw. Mitch twisted just in time to avoid the blow. Then he delivered a swift kick to the back of the man's knees, causing him to crumple to the floor.

Mitch's early education in street fighting was only enhanced by the combat moves he'd been taught when he'd gone into law enforcement. This loser wasn't going to win this fight. Mitch just hoped the guy would be smart enough to figure that out before Mitch really had to hurt him.

No such luck.

By the time Mitch had scraped the guy off the floor and dumped him in the back of a taxicab, the two woman who had been fighting were back on the dance floor once more, with two new guys.

Donna Cummings, a blond waitress with an eternal wad of gum in her mouth sidled up to him. "You look like you could use a drink, Mitch."

He rubbed his knuckles. "I could use a night off, but I'll settle for a drink. Make it the usual. In fact, make it a double."

She grinned. "One grape soda coming up."

Mitch walked back to his post at the door, sensing that it was going to be another long night. He'd rather be watching a Clint Eastwood marathon on television. Anything but hanging around a bunch of lonely, desperate people trying to find love.

What really disgusted him was that he used to be one of them. Trolling the bars for women had been one of his favorite hobbies. His friends had joked that he must be related to Sam Malone, the famous womanizer on *Cheers*. But in the last year or so, that lifestyle had lost its appeal.

He'd successfully avoided the flirtations and not-so-subtle invitations of the women patrons of The Jungle during his first two weeks on the job. By now most of the regulars knew he was off-limits. Although Donna, recently married and ready to confine everyone she met to that institution, still tried to play matchmaker.

"Here you go," she said, handing him a drink. "Did you see the blonde at the bar? She's cute."

"Too skinny for my taste," he said.

"You're too picky," Donna said. "Why don't you try to find a nice woman, Mitch? Someone who can make you happy."

"Women are like potato chips," he said with a smile. "I can't stop at just one."

She rolled her eyes. "Potato chips?"

"Maybe I should have said M&M's."

"Maybe you should quit trying to con me, Mitch Malone. I think you're one of those old-fashioned romantics, the type I never see in this place anymore. You actually want more from a woman than her body."

Mitch shook his head. "Donna, you've got me all wrong. I'm a connoisseur of the female body. The only reason I work here is because of the view." He motioned to the scantily clad women on the dance floor. "I get a great show every night."

Donna folded her arms across her chest. "Then why don't you ever take one of them home?"

"I would, but my place is a mess."

She laughed. "As if any woman in her right mind would care. You're a romantic, Mitch, just admit it."

"I plead the fifth."

She shook her head. "You're impossible."

Time to go to work. "Hey, that's better than desperate. Actually though, I hear this is the place to score some help in the romance department. Some of the guys I've talked to come here to pick up bootleg Viagra, hoping to boost their...vitality."

Her eyes widened. "Really? Who?"

He shrugged. "I didn't get any names." Then he grinned. "Why, does you new husband need a boost?"

"Hardly," she huffed, then smiled. "I have no complaints in that department."

He nodded, then looked around the bar. He was walking a thin line, trying to gain information without arousing suspicion. "I may have to give the stuff a try sometime. See what happens."

Her brows rose. "Couldn't that be dangerous?"

"Exhausting, maybe. But not dangerous."

"Still, it's illegal. No silly drug is worth going to jail." Then she turned and walked back to the bar.

Mitch mentally crossed Donna's name off his list of suspects. She hadn't taken the bait. He didn't like deceiving her or the other employees of The Jungle. But if he wanted to succeed in his investigation, subterfuge was part of the job.

Still, he stuck to the real facts about his life as much as possible. He'd told people he'd grown up on the streets, raised by his grandmother after his parents abandoned him when he was nine years old. He admitted that he'd gotten into some trouble as a juvenile and received his Graduation Equivalency Diploma. What he left out, though, was the cop who had been his boxing coach, a man who had steered him into a career in law enforcement. But absolute truth was simply a luxury Mitch couldn't afford right now.

The sound of a glass breaking broke his reverie. He looked toward the bar and saw a beer mug laying in pieces on the floor. A sudden stillness came over the room, though music still blared from the jukebox. The lights from the disco ball glittered over an empty dance floor. Most of the patrons were staring at the door. He followed their gazes and saw an eerily familiar woman standing just inside the room.

He stared at her and swallowed hard. His gaze took in everything at once. The long toffee-brown hair, the big brown eyes, and the modest curves that shouldn't make a man stare—but they did. His eyes fell to the short, tight black skirt that revealed a pair of incredible legs. He blinked and looked again. The skirt was so sheer, he could damn well see through it! Heat kindled low and spread through his body like a brushfire.

It was the woman from the back alley, though he

couldn't remember her name. Hell, he could barely remember his own name. But he knew what to call her as soon as she started walking toward him.

Trouble.

4

THE BLACK SKIRT CARESSED Claire's thighs as she walked into The Jungle. She was intrigued by the odd sense of power it gave her. The way the silky fabric molded to her body. She loved the way it made her legs seem longer and her hips slimmer. But most of all, she loved the smolder of desire she saw in Mitch's eyes. Eyes that looked even bluer than she remembered.

Unfortunately, he wore a shirt tonight. It was a black T-shirt, stretched a little taut at the shoulders, with the name of the nightclub emblazoned across it in white letters. And it was accompanied by a pair of snug black denim jeans. Mitch Malone didn't need any magic clothes to make her smolder.

He watched her approach him, his gaze trickling down her body like warm syrup.

"Hello," she said, holding out her hand. She'd better get used to approaching strange men if she wanted this study to be a success. "I'm Claire Dellafield."

"Claire," he echoed, in a way that told her he'd remember it this time. His hand swallowed hers whole and a delicious zing shot through her body. According to her initial observations, the skirt was definitely causing a chemical reaction.

So far, both Mitch and her cabdriver seemed to be affected. The cabdriver had even followed her into the nightclub.

"Hey, babe," the man now called from the doorway in a thick Bronx accent. "Wait up."

He was obviously making good on his pledge to follow her to the ends of the earth. But there was one place he couldn't go.

She smiled up at Mitch. "Could you please direct me to the ladies' room?"

He didn't say anything, just hitched his thumb over her shoulder, pointing toward the corner of the nightclub.

"Thank you," she murmured, circling around him and walking briskly in that direction. Claire quickened her pace as the cabdriver's voice carried over the room. The man was certainly persistent. He'd screeched to a stop at the corner where her apartment stood, kicked out his irate passenger, then promised her a free ride.

She'd thought he meant in his taxicab.

But he'd made his intentions quite clear when he'd pulled up to The Jungle. She'd turned him down. Then he'd tried to sweeten the offer by promising to let her tie him up. The conversation had gone downhill from there. And now she was forced to hide in the bathroom. Maybe the skirt had some drawbacks after all.

Claire slipped into the empty ladies' room, wondering how long she'd have to stay here before the cabbie finally gave up and went away.

But she underestimated him.

The cabbie barreled through the door, his narrow face lighting up when he saw her. "Are we playing hide-and-seek?"

Claire planted her hands on her hips. "I think you missed the sign on the door. It's for women only."

"Let's continue the game at my place," he offered, taking another step closer. "I'll let you hide in my bed."

"I'm not going anywhere with you,' she said firmly. "I don't even know your name."

His thin lips curved into a smile. "My girlfriends call me the Love Stallion."

"Well, Mr. Stallion, I'm flattered by your interest, but I'm working at the moment."

He gaze flicked over her body. "I'll pay top dollar for a woman like you."

She blinked. "Top dollar? You think I'm a prostitute?"

"I think you're my greatest fantasy." He took another step closer. "One I want to enjoy all night long."

Claire slipped her hand inside her purse, curling her fingers around the pepper spray A.J. had given her in case of an emergency. "I'm going to count to three. If you're not gone by the time I'm done, you're going to regret it."

"Why?" He grinned. "Are you going to spank me?"

"One."

He licked his lips. "You are so hot."

"Two."

He raised one cocky eyebrow. "Playing hard to get? Give me a break. A woman like you? In a skirt like that?"

"This is your last chance," she warned, pulling the canister out of her purse and taking careful aim.

The door to the rest room swung open and Mitch stepped inside. His gaze swung from the pepper spray in Claire's hand to the man standing in front of her. "I hope I'm not interrupting anything."

Claire shook her head. "He was just leaving."

"I'm not going anywhere without you," the cabbie announced.

"Think again." Mitch folded his arms across his broad chest. "I want you out of here. Now."

The cabbie stuck out his jaw. "And if I don't feel like leaving?"

Mitch's blue eyes narrowed. "Then you're going to feel my fist shoved down your throat."

Claire stepped between them, feeling somewhat responsible. After all, this entire situation was because of the skirt. "I don't want to cause any trouble."

"Too late," Mitch muttered, then took a menacing step toward the cabdriver.

"All right," the cabbie said, backing up. "I'm leaving." Then he turned to Claire. "But I'll be parked right outside waiting for you, babe."

"Thanks for the warning," Claire called after him. Then she looked at Mitch, who was scowling at her. "What?"

"Next time, leave your boyfriend problems at the door."

Her eyes widened at his curt tone. Had the skirt lost its effect already? *"Boyfriend problems?* That creep isn't my boyfriend. He was my cabdriver."

"Did you forget to pay the fare?"

"He refused to let me pay him anything. He almost refused to let me out of his cab." She moved around him toward the door. "Now if you'll excuse me...."

But Mitch stepped in front of her, blocking the path. He was so close she could see a small scar just below his chin and smell the hint of aftershave he wore. His formidable size should have intimidated her. But she knew instinctively he wouldn't hurt her. In fact, for one fleeting second, she thought he might move even closer. Her skin prickled at the thought and the skirt seemed almost hot against her skin.

She craned her neck to look up at him. He just stared at her for a long moment before finally stepping out of her way. "Enjoy your evening."

"Thank you." She walked out of the ladies' room and took a deep breath. Funny how she found it hard to breathe all of a sudden. Maybe it was the scented air freshener in the ladies' room. *Or the glint of desire in*

Mitch's blue eyes. The next moment, he stood right behind her, his heat caressing her neck.

"When you're ready to leave," he growled in her ear, "just let me know. I'll help you get another cab."

She turned to face him. "That won't be necessary."

"I insist." Then he turned and walked away.

Claire stared after him, realizing she'd never had that kind of effect on a man before. It was intoxicating. Especially after the way he'd dismissed her in the alley behind The Jungle two weeks ago.

But she wasn't here to impress Mitch Malone. It was time to line up volunteers for her research project. Several men were seated at stools by the bar, where a man with too much gray hair peeking through his muscle shirt stood behind the counter barking orders at a harried bartender.

Where to begin? Claire had read her father's study numerous times, as well as his copious notes. Marcus Dellafield had introduced himself to several patrons before carefully selecting ten of them to be the main focus of his research. All the test subjects had been women. Claire planned to reverse the study and focus on men this time.

She slid onto the last empty bar stool, setting her purse in her lap. Several stools squeaked as men turned to look at her.

"Ask the lady what she wants to drink," the man with the thick, gray chest hair growled behind the bar.

A harried young bartender hurried over to her. "What can I get you?"

"I'll have a glass of wine," she said, deciding to keep it simple for him. "Merlot, if you have it."

The bartender looked at the older man. "Do we have it?"

"Hell, yes." He pointed to one of the lower shelves. "Second bottle from the right."

The bartender set a bottle on top of the counter.

"That's pinot grigio, not merlot, you idiot!"

"I love pinot grigio!" Claire exclaimed, then smiled at the red-faced bartender. "You must have read my mind."

"Get the lady a glass," the older man ordered gruffly, then he turned to Claire. "You must be new in town."

"How can you tell?"

"You're too nice. Besides, I've been running this place for the last thirty years. I can spot a tourist a mile away."

"Thirty years?" Claire echoed. "Then maybe you remember my father, Marcus Dellafield. He conducted a research study here called *Strangers in the Night* about twenty-five years ago. I'm his daughter, Claire."

The bartender's scowl faded into something that could almost be called a smile. "Well, hell. Of course, I remember Marc. I'm Dick Vandalay, owner of The Jungle."

Marc? She'd never heard anyone call her father that

before. Somehow it didn't seem to fit with his dignified image. But her father had been a relatively young man back then. Handsome, too, from the photographs she'd seen. Her throat tightened and she had to swallow hard to keep from choking on a sob. She reached for her glass of wine and took a long sip.

"I haven't heard from Marc for a while." He looked around the bar. "Did he come with you?"

"My father passed away nine months ago," she said softly as tears pricked her eyes.

He pushed a paper napkin toward her. "Aw, hell, kid. I'm sorry."

"It's all right," she assured him with a watery smile. "I'm just glad I finally get to meet the man I've heard so much about."

"Marc was a hell of a guy," Dick said, then glanced at his new bartender. "You don't add tequila to a Bloody Mary, you idiot!" He strode to the far end of the bar. "Are you trying to put me out of business?"

From the looks of the place, that wouldn't be hard to do. Claire let her gaze drift around the nightclub, noting the deep gauges on the oak bar, the water stains on the ceiling and the red shag carpet lining the walls. It certainly didn't resemble the trendy hotspot her father had described.

Frankly, the place looked like a dump.

But that would only make her study more interesting. She could do a comparative study of the clientele, then and now. Claire crossed her legs, then noticed the man seated next to her staring at them. "Hello," she said cordially. "Do you come here often?"

"Not often enough," he said, dragging his gaze to her face, "since I've never seen you here before."

"My name is Claire Dellafield." She reached inside her purse and drew out a business card. "Are you a regular here?"

"Every night of the week," he replied with a grin.

"Would you be interested in participating in a research study on human mating behavior?"

"With you? Absolutely."

"Wonderful." She pulled out a pen and paper. "What's your name?"

"Albert Ramirez."

She jotted it down. "I'll need your telephone number, too, so I can contact you for an interview. My cellular phone number is on that business card, in case you need to reach me in the meantime."

He wrinkled his forehead as he stared at her card. "You're an anthropologist?"

"That's right. And I want to thank you for volunteering to be my first subject."

His eyes moved back to her legs. "No. *Thank you.*"

His tone told her he wanted to do more than volunteer for the study, but before she could set him straight, another man at the bar leaned forward.

"Hey, I'd like to volunteer, too."

"Hey, sign me up, too." echoed a third deep voice as more men crowded around the bar.

Claire reached in her purse for a handful of business cards. *Mission accomplished.*

MITCH COULDN'T TAKE HIS eyes off of her, a problem he obviously shared with most of the men in the place. A small mob of them had formed around her bar stool. He stood at his post near the door, wondering if he should find some excuse to break things up.

Most of the women in the place had left, disgruntled by the sudden lack of male attention. But not one man had walked out the door.

Donna appeared at his side. "How about another grape soda?"

"No, thanks."

She followed his gaze, then frowned. "I'm surprised Dick allowed a working girl in here."

"Working girl?" he echoed. "She's not a hooker." He was as certain of that as he was that the sky was blue somewhere above the smog.

Donna snorted. "Then why is she handing out business cards and telling all the guys she's looking for volunteers to study *human mating behavior?*"

A call girl? Every instinct told him no way. But he couldn't deny that she definitely knew how to arouse a man's baser instincts. Mitch clenched his jaw, realizing he'd let a woman distract him. Again. But he couldn't get rid of her. *Or could he?*

He looked toward the bar, noting for the first time that Vandalay was nowhere in sight. The new apprentice bartender was filling drink orders. "Where is Dick?"

"Out back having a smoke."

Mitch nodded, then pushed himself off the wall. "Fine. Then I'll take care of the problem."

Donna smiled her relief. "Thanks, Mitch."

He walked toward the bar, arriving just as a brawl broke out between several of the men gathered there. He ducked as a bar stool flew over his head, smashing several bottles. Alcohol fumes permeated the air as beer mugs crashed to the floor.

"Break it up," he bellowed, separating the two men nearest to him. He saw Claire climb onto the bar, swinging her legs out of the way just as one man shoved another against the counter.

Mitch caught a hard fist in the ribs, then shot his elbow out to neutralize his attacker. It connected and he heard bone crunch.

"Everybody back off," Mitch declared, shoving men out of the way until he formed a barrier between Claire and her admirers. The new bartender crouched under the counter.

Mitch turned to look at the woman who had caused all this trouble and saw that she was standing on the bar now, that black skirt backlit by the neon lights above. His mouth went dry, as he stood there, mesmerized by the almost transparent skirt.

Then someone jostled against him, trying to get closer. Mitch shoved him back, hearing the crunch of broken glass under his shoes. He glared at the men still crowded around him, muttering angrily among themselves at his interference.

"You guys hard of hearing?" Mitch folded his arms across his chest. "Did you happen to see what happened to the last guy who didn't hear so well? He won't be dancing for a while. Now I'll say it one more time, nice and slow. Back. Off."

He stared down several of the men. One by one, they peeled away from the group and headed out the door, including the new bartender. Soon Mitch and Claire were alone.

He wrapped his arms around her legs and pulled her off the bar.

"What do you think you're doing?" she asked, struggling in his arms. But she was no match for him.

"Funny," he replied, letting her slide down his body until her face was even with his. But he was tall enough that her feet still didn't touch the floor. "I was about to ask you the very same question."

"I'm trying to get some work done here."

He liked the golden sparks he saw in her big brown eyes. And hated the fact that he'd noticed. "Work that just happens to be illegal in the state of New York. Just consider yourself lucky that I haven't called the cops. Yet."

"Called the cops?" She looked at him like he was crazy. "What for?"

"Soliciting."

Her jaw sagged. "You're as deranged as Mr. Stallion!"

"Is that the name of your pimp?"

She shook her head. "I don't have a pimp. And I'm not a prostitute. For your information, I'm an anthropologist."

He shook his head. "And here I thought I'd heard it all. I'll give you points for originality."

Her nostrils flared. "It happens to be the truth! If you'll just let me explain..."

"Why don't we save time by just having you answer a few questions. Were you or were you not handing out business cards with your telephone number?"

"Yes," she replied, nodding toward one of her cards still lying on the bar. "You can see it for yourself."

He moved a step, still holding her in his arms. He told himself it was to keep her under control, but he couldn't deny the pleasure it gave him to feel her flesh pressed close against him. Reaching out his left hand, he picked up the card. "Claire Dellafield. Anthropologist."

"I told you." She tilted her chin. "I'm conducting a research study on human mating behavior. I was simply looking for potential volunteers...."

"Right." He wrapped his left arm back around her, then carried her toward the door. "Time to go, Claire."

Her brown eyes widened. "Go where?"

He inhaled her delicate scent. "I'm kicking you out of here before you cause any more trouble."

She struggled in his arms. "You're the one making a scene."

"Hold still," he ordered, his body reacting to her gyrations. If she wasn't so much trouble, she'd be just his type. Feisty and round in all the right places. "I'm just doing my job."

"Is it your job to harass paying customers?"

Mitch snorted, as he turned and backed out the door. "You haven't bought a drink all night. Your admirers couldn't get their wallets out fast enough."

"This is a singles club, isn't it? Is it unusual for the patrons to buy drinks for each other?"

She had a point, but Mitch wasn't about to concede. Not when she'd started a brawl within half an hour of her arrival. Not when her antics threatened to distract him from his investigation. Not when he had an almost irresistible urge to kiss her sassy mouth.

She arched a finely winged brow. "Well?"

He carried Claire to the curb, ignoring the frantic honking of her lovelorn cabbie. Then he loosened his grip, allowing her to slide the rest of the way down his body. Sweet torture.

"Enjoying yourself?" she challenged, her feet now firmly on the ground.

"I like it better when you don't talk," he said, his body throbbing.

She narrowed her eyes. "Just try to stop me."

So he did. The only way he knew. Mitch lowered his head and captured her sassy mouth with his own. Blood rushed south as her mouth softened in surprise. He deepened the kiss, knowing she'd pull back at any moment. Only she didn't.

What the hell was wrong with him? With her?

He finally broke the kiss, then stepped back before she could slap him—even though he deserved it.

She stared up at him, lifting her fingers to her red lips. "Why did you do that?"

"I'm through answering questions." Mitch hailed a taxi with a female driver.

"Then let me go back in The Jungle!"

He shook his head. "Lady, you've been causing trouble since you walked through the door. First, I had to kick one of your admirers out of the ladies' rest room. Then I had to break up that mob surrounding you. This is my turf and we play by my rules. They're very simple. Two strikes and you're out."

"You're serious, aren't you?"

"Damn straight I'm serious," Mitch replied as the taxi pulled up to the curb. "You're pretty bright for an anthropologist."

"I'll have you know I've never been kicked out of a bar in my life!"

"Then this will be fun new experience for you." He opened the back door, but Claire didn't move.

"I want to speak to the owner."

"He's occupied at the moment." Mitch moved closer to her, backing her toward the cab. "But I'll be happy to give him a message."

She fell back onto the rear seat of the cab, then

swung her legs inside, probably afraid he was going to maul her again. "Tell him I'll be back."

"Over my dead body."

"Whatever." Then she slammed the taxicab door in his face.

He watched the cab drive off into the night, breathing a deep sigh of relief. What had come over him? He'd never handled a woman like that before. His brain was glad she was gone, but his body still wanted her back. Maybe it was this awful heat. As a cop, he knew the crime rate soared with the temperature. Maybe the heat was having some kind of strange effect on his hormones.

As Mitch walked back into the nightclub, he noticed he still held her business card—with her cell phone number on it. He hesitated a moment, then ripped it into tiny pieces.

He'd been tempted enough for one night.

5

THE NEXT MORNING, CLAIRE awoke slowly, wincing at the bright June sunlight streaming in through the window.

"Good morning."

She stifled a scream as her gaze fell on a figure sitting on the end of her bed. "Petra!"

Petra beamed at her. "Hello, my angel."

Claire struggled to sit up, her long hair falling in her face. She pushed it out of the way. "What are you doing in here?"

"I'm welcoming you to New York City! Now come over and give me a hug."

Claire leaned forward and wrapped her arms around the woman who had been the closest thing to a mother she'd ever known. Closing her eyes, she inhaled Petra's familiar and comforting sandalwood scent.

Though in her early sixties, Petra had the figure of a woman half her age and regularly participated in 5K runs around the country. This morning Petra wore neon orange spandex running shorts and a matching crop top. Her white hair was layered in a flattering pixie cut and tears shone in her bright green eyes.

"I'm so glad you're here," Petra said, cupping Claire's face in her hands. "You look wonderful."

Claire smiled. "I've seen myself in the mirror first thing in the morning. Wonderful definitely isn't the adjective I would use."

"That's only because you never give yourself enough credit. You're every bit as pretty as those two roommates of yours."

Claire pulled back in surprise. "When did you meet A.J. and Sam?"

"I haven't officially met them," Petra replied. "Not yet. But I did peek into their rooms this morning while I was searching for you. They look quite nice. Although it is a little hard to tell when they're asleep."

"They *are* nice," Claire confirmed. "But they would have been terrified if they'd woken up and saw a stranger standing by their bed."

"I'm not a stranger," Petra replied, with a dismissive wave of her hand. "I'm the next-door neighbor. I didn't get in from Bermuda until very late last night and simply couldn't wait another minute to see you."

"Well, you should have at least knocked. How *did* you get in here, anyway?"

"Franco gave me a passkey. I'm so sorry I wasn't here when you arrived in the city, Claire. I completely misplaced the date of your arrival."

"That's all right," Claire told her. "I managed just fine on my own."

"So I see." Petra beamed at her. "I knew you could

find a way to win Tavish's McLain's apartment." She reached out to brush a stray curl off Claire's forehead. You're so smart and pretty."

Claire laughed. "And you're so biased."

"I'm the model of objectivity," her godmother informed her. "You just don't have enough confidence in your own abilities."

Claire sighed as she leaned back against the pillows. "After last night, I have even less."

"What happened last night?"

Where should she start? "My research study at The Jungle started and ended last night. I got kicked out of the nightclub."

Petra's eyebrows rose an inch. "How intriguing. I can't wait to hear this story."

"It was humiliating." Claire propped another pillow behind her head. "This big, macho bouncer named Mitch decided I was causing too much trouble. When I think about him..." She grunted in frustration, her hands curling into fists, "I just want to hit something."

"Big and macho?" Petra mused. "I like him already."

Claire shook her head, letting all her emotions from last night build up again. "He was a total jerk. First, he manhandles me, literally carrying me out of the nightclub. Then the man has the audacity to kiss me!"

"Did you kiss him back?"

Claire hesitated. "It surprised me. I might have at first. A little."

"So he wasn't totally repulsive?"

"I never said he was repulsive," Claire replied, remembering those vivid blue eyes. "I suppose you could even call him handsome if you like the cave-dweller type."

"Illustrate him for me."

Claire was used to this unusual request. As an artist, Petra always wanted very specific details to place the image in her mind's eye. She loved to use words as a palette to describe the people around her. Her eulogy for Marcus Dellafield had painted him as a man of beauty, vision and unconditional love for his only daughter.

"Mitch's eyes are blue," Claire began, trying to remain objective, "like the morning glories Dad used to plant in the window boxes."

"What about his hair?"

"Thick and dark. Like hot fudge. His skin was smooth but tanned, with little wrinkles around the corners of his eyes when he smiles. Not that he did much smiling at me."

Claire closed her eyes, picturing Mitch in her mind. "He wore all black, from his T-shirt to his black denim jeans to his black running shoes. If he wasn't so tanned, he would have looked completely washed out. His teeth were very white, though. I'll bet he had them capped."

Petra gave her a knowing smile. "It certainly sounds as if you've hardly been thinking about him at all."

"I have been thinking about pressing assault charges against him." Claire's skin tingled at the memory of sliding down his hard body. She'd hated every minute of it. Really. "He was holding me so tightly I probably have bruises."

Petra crossed her legs. "So this man threw you out of The Jungle, did he?"

"He picked me up off the bar and refused to put me down until he reached the sidewalk."

Petra's brow crinkled. "What were you doing on the bar?"

"There was a fight, but it didn't last long." *Thanks to Mitch.* "Anyway, the man wouldn't listen to reason. Or even let me explain why I was there."

"I think he sounds yummy."

"Yummy? I don't think you understand." Claire inhaled deeply. "Mitch Malone is a bully. He's smug and arrogant and self-righteous. Plus, he always thinks he's right."

Petra smiled. "And he's made you experience something I will venture you've never experienced before."

"What?" Claire asked warily.

"Passion."

Claire swallowed. "I'm here to study passion, not experience it."

"Can't you do both?"

The idea appealed to her more than she wanted to admit. "I'm a teacher," she began, "I have certain standards to maintain."

"Maybe back at Penleigh," Petra interjected. "Here in New York City, you're a young, beautiful single girl. Why not embrace life in all its messy glory? I know it was difficult for you growing up on campus. Everyone expected the daughter of Marcus Dellafield to be above reproach. And you were. Marcus was so proud of you."

Claire's throat tightened. "And I was proud of him."

"I know," Petra replied softly. "But now you have a chance to really experience life. I've read between the lines in all those letters you sent me, Claire. You named all the reasons why you weren't certain you could recreate Marcus's research study except the real one."

Claire lifted her chin a notch. "Which is?"

"You've got no practical experience in human mating behavior yourself."

"That's not true," Claire retorted. "I've dated several times."

"Under the watchful eye of every student and professor at Penleigh. Campus life is so different from the real world. You've been insulated there. Sheltered." Petra rose to her feet and whirled around the room. "Now is your chance to emerge from that cocoon and fly."

No one could ever accuse Petra Gerard of not having passion.

"I'm not afraid of flying," Claire said. "But I'd like to have a destination."

"No, no, no!" Petra moved back toward the bed. "It's the journey that's important. The jump off the cliff into the great unknown."

"So basically you're saying I should have a wild, romantic fling while I'm here for the summer."

"Exactly."

Claire grew thoughtful. "I'm not opposed to romance. But I intend to concentrate on my career first. I should have a couple of weeks free this summer after I complete my research project.

Petra groaned as she sank back down on the bed. "You can't pencil passion in on your calendar. You must pursue it. Or rather, him."

Claire shook her head. "If you're referring to Mitch, forget it."

"Why not? He sounds delicious."

Claire sighed. "Because he's not attracted to me."

Petra arched an eyebrow. "So why did he kiss you?"

"Because of the skirt. When I'm not wearing it, he doesn't even know I exist."

Petra looked extremely curious. Now she'd done it, Claire thought.

"Let's rewind for a moment. What is this skirt you're talking about?" Petra asked.

"The skirt is the reason Sam and A.J. and I were able to convince McLain to sublet us his apartment. It belongs to Sam and it's supposed to have some thread spun from a rare island root that draws men like a magnet."

Petra looked thoughtful. "Sounds handy."

Claire nodded. "I wore it to The Jungle last night to attract men for my research study. And it worked. I was virtually mobbed by males of every shape, size and color. Until Mitch kicked me out."

"Maybe he was jealous."

Claire hadn't considered that possibility. "He didn't seem jealous."

"Men are complex creatures," Petra informed her. "That's why I like to spend so much time with them. Well, that and the great sex." Petra had never been reticent about discussing her active social life. Her last boyfriend had been a thirty-seven-year-old bricklayer. "But I digress. Now, what can I do to help you?"

"I have to find a way to get back into The Jungle. I made several promising contacts last night. I need to follow up on them before they lose interest."

"So what's the problem?"

"Mitch Malone. He told me never to darken the doorway of the nightclub again."

"Ah, an ultimatum." Petra's eyes flashed with amusement. "Then you must return. He'll be expecting you."

Claire shook her head. "You don't understand. He meant it."

Petra laughed. "Oh, Claire, I sculpt naked men for a living. I understand them much better than you think."

"Naked men?" Claire said, realizing her god-mother was serious. "Since when?

"I started six months ago and now I just can't seem to stop. There's something so...stimulating about the male body. Don't you think?"

Unfortunately, Claire didn't have enough personal experience to express an opinion. Maybe Petra was right. Maybe it *was* time to add a little passion to her life.

For a fleeting moment, Claire pictured Mitch naked and a flash of heat rippled through her. "So you think I should just walk right back into The Jungle and pre-tend nothing ever happened?"

"Absolutely. What's the worst thing he can do?"

"Just kick me out again." Her skin tingled at the possibility.

"But perhaps he won't. Perhaps he'll admire a woman who challenges him."

Claire had her doubts about that. But if she left the skirt at home this time, he couldn't accuse her of caus-ing trouble. Men had never mobbed her before last night. Mitch might not even notice her this time.

But was that really what she wanted?

"All right," Claire announced, forcing thoughts of Mitch out of her mind. "One way or another, I'll find my way back into The Jungle."

Petra clapped her hands together. "Let the mating games begin."

MITCH LOOKED AROUND THE nightclub, bracing him-self for another busy Saturday night. Latin music pounded from the sound system and several couples headed for the dance floor. The owner, Dick Vandalay, stood behind the bar, taking inventory of the stock.

For some reason, Mitch felt restless tonight. Maybe it was the frustration, waiting for Vandalay to finally make a move. Or the monotony of seeing the same faces night after night. Or the fact that he kept expecting Claire Dellafield to walk through the door.

That was the problem. Part of him wanted to see her again. The part south of his brain. Maybe this temporary vow of celibacy was affecting his sanity. The sooner he closed this case and moved on, the better.

Vandalay hailed him from the bar. Mitch pushed himself off the wall and threaded his way through the crowd.

"Do you need something?"

"We're short on scotch and bourbon," Vandalay replied. "Bring up a couple of bottles of each from the basement. Some tequila, too."

Mitch nodded, then headed for the stairwell. It was dark and musty, lit only by a single bare bulb. The wooden steps creaked as he descended into the dank basement. His mind flashed to Elaine and the fall she'd taken at that abandoned building. It had been broad daylight. If only she'd seen who pushed her.

Another question without an answer. Yet. After grabbing the bottles, he returned to the main floor and carried the liquor to the bar. Only Vandalay wasn't there anymore. Mitch looked around the room until he spotted him sitting at a corner table with a petite redhead.

She was cute. With big brown eyes and a supple mouth. Nice curves, too. Familiar curves.

Mitch narrowed his gaze. She wouldn't dare. *Would she?*

"Grape soda, Mitch?"

He turned to see Donna standing at his elbow. "No thanks." Then he nodded toward the corner of the nightclub. "See anything odd there?"

Dinna's brow furrowed. "What do you mean?"

"The redhead. Does she look familiar?"

Donna shrugged. "Not really. She asked to see Vandalay. I figured she wanted to apply for a job."

Mitch kept staring at her. "I don't think she wants a job. That's the same woman who was in here last night claiming to be an anthropologist."

Donna looked surprised. "The one you kicked out?"

He nodded. "Claire Dellafield."

Donna studied her for a long moment. "I think you're right. Nice wig. But I guess Ms. Dellafield didn't get the message the first time."

"Guess not," Mitch replied still staring at her. "Maybe I should find out why she's really here."

"How are you going to do that?"

"I'll think of something," Mitch said as he walked over to the table.

Claire obviously saw him coming, because she

quickly leaned forward and began talking nonstop to Vandalay. Mitch's heart rate picked up in preparation for battle.

Only this was one fight he didn't intend to lose.

6

A LARGE SHADOW FELL across the table, but Claire didn't look away from Dick Vandalay. If she could convince him that her research project would be good for business, Mitch Malone wouldn't dare kick her out again.

"My plan is to revisit the study that my father did here twenty-five years ago," Claire explained. "A study that I'm hoping will bring The Jungle as much free publicity now as it did then."

"There's only one problem," Mitch intoned, as Vandalay finally seemed to notice him standing there. "It might not be the kind of publicity that will be good for business."

Vandalay's bushy gray brows drew together. "What do you mean?"

Mitch nodded toward Claire. "This is the woman who started that brawl last night."

Vandalay's gray eyes widened. "You?"

"I didn't start anything," Claire said indignantly. "A couple of men had too much to drink and got out of control. I'm sure I could have handled the situation if your bouncer, here, hadn't interfered."

"My interference saved your pretty little butt," Mitch retorted.

Claire was determined not to lose her temper. "I'd prefer it if you'd keep my butt out of this conversation."

"Hold it." Vandalay held up both hands, then looked up at Mitch. "Donna told me you had to kick a woman out of here last night. Are you telling me Claire is that woman?"

"One and the same," Mitch replied. "Only she was a brunette last night, not a redhead." He turned to her. "Did you really think that wig would fool me?"

But she ignored him, focusing her attention on Vandalay. "I was hoping it would fool him just long enough to give me a chance to talk to you. That brawl last night was unfortunate, but I can promise you nothing like that will ever happen again."

"Right," Mitch scoffed. "I don't suppose you happened to mention the incident in the ladies' rest room?"

"Rest room?" Vandalay echoed, looking back and forth between the two of them.

"That was nothing," she assured him. "The important thing is that I've already lined up all the volunteers for my research project. I'll conduct in-depth interviews with all ten of them, but I also need to observe them in action at The Jungle."

"You plan to interview them here?" Vandalay asked.

"No," Claire replied. "I believe it would be more

valuable for me to see each subject in his home environment. Get a sense of his/her personal lives to compare and contrast it to his/her behavior in a social setting."

"You're going to walk into the homes of ten strangers?" Vandalay asked.

"Don't you think that's a little dangerous?" Mitch interjected.

"My research doesn't have to be done in their homes," Claire replied, still keeping her focus on Vandalay. "I could meet them in a restaurant or any other public place. And I do carry pepper spray in my purse."

"It sure didn't do you much good last night." Mitch flashed a smile. "Good thing I was there to save your pretty little butt again."

Vandalay sighed. "Hell, Claire. You know how much I liked your old man, but Marc knew how to handle himself in place like this. It's not the same for a woman."

"My point exactly," Mitch said.

"That's ridiculous," Claire said flatly, then drew in a deep breath. "I understand your concerns, Mr. Vandalay, but I think the potential gains for your nightclub far outweigh any risks."

Vandalay hesitated. "This place could use some free advertising, that's for damn sure."

Mitch shook his head. "That advertising might be a headline that reads Anthropologist Attacked While Researching The Jungle."

Claire clenched her jaw, wondering if Mitch was truly concerned about her safety or just miffed that she'd gone over his head. "That's not going to happen."

"Maybe not," Vandalay admitted. "But I have an idea that I think will make us all happy."

Claire enjoyed watching Mitch's smile fade. "I'm certainly open to compromise."

"Good." Vandalay hitched his thumb toward the bouncer. "I'll have Malone keep an eye on you, both here and at those interviews."

Claire's mouth fell open. She closed it again, then shook her head. "I really don't think that's necessary."

"Neither do I," Mitch said bluntly.

"Hell, Malone, I'll make it worth your while," Vandalay promised. "You've already proven you can take care of the lady. I'd consider it a personal favor. And I always repay favors."

Mitch hesitated, giving Claire a chance to jump in. "I'm afraid he might get bored. The field of cultural anthropology can be pretty complex."

"I can always bring my coloring books," Mitch quipped.

"You two can work out the details," Vandalay replied. "As long as you both understand that I'm not about to let Marc's daughter run around this city unprotected."

Claire didn't like his terms, but at this point she'd

take what she could get. "I guess that sounds reasonable to me."

"Not to me," Mitch bit out. "I hired on as a bouncer, not a baby-sitter."

Vandalay scowled up at him. "Don't give me grief on this. You'll get paid for your time. If you don't like the damn terms, you can quit right now and I'll find another bouncer to take your place."

Claire saw a muscle flex in Mitch's jaw. He was not at all happy with Vandalay's ultimatum. Served him right for turning all macho on her last night. But did she really want to spend the next few weeks in his company? Especially if he thought he could still tell her what to do?

Time to make Mr. Vandalay a counter offer. One that she knew would appeal to him.

"There might be another problem," she began slowly.

Vandalay turned to her. "Let's hear it."

"It's important that the subjects in my study don't feel uncomfortable during the interviews, which they might if Mitch is there as my bodyguard."

"So?"

She leaned forward. "So how about if I hire Mitch as my research assistant? I have just enough grant money to cover the extra expense, if he's willing to settle for minimum wage. Then it won't cost you anything, Mr. Vandalay, because Mitch will be my employee."

Mitch gaped at her. "Are you crazy?"

Claire was starting to wonder. She had to be crazy to even consider such an arrangement. But Dick Vandalay wasn't leaving her much choice. If she wanted to conduct her research project at The Jungle, then Mitch Malone was part of the bargain.

"Rule number one," she told him. "Never argue with the boss."

Mitch opened his mouth, then snapped it shut again before spinning on his heel and walking away.

She watched him go, noting that he had a pretty little butt himself.

No doubt about it—she'd won round one.

MITCH STOOD IN THE gloomy basement of The Jungle and punched out Elaine's number on his cell phone. She'd been released from the hospital today and he hated to bother her on her first day home, but this was an emergency.

"Hello?"

It didn't surprise him that Elaine answered the phone herself. She wasn't the type to play helpless invalid—even if she did fit the part.

"It's Mitch."

"Hey, partner, what's up?"

"We've got a problem." He took a deep breath, trying to decide where to start. "An anthropologist walked into The Jungle last night...."

"Since when did you start telling dumb jokes?" she interjected.

"This isn't a joke." Then he told her the whole

story. "So now Claire Dellafield's planning to do the same research project that made her father famous twenty-five years ago. And somehow I've been roped into helping her."

"And if you refuse?"

"Then I'm out of here." He rubbed one hand over the back of his neck. "And the woman obviously needs someone to watch out for her. I just don't want that someone to be me—I already have a job to do. Make that two jobs."

"What did you say her name was again?"

"Dellafield." He glanced up at the top of the stairs to make certain the door was still firmly closed. "Claire Dellafield."

"Hold on."

Mitch heard the phone hit the floor, then Elaine's husband yelling at her to get back in bed. Several moments later she was back on the line, excitement bubbling in her voice. "Here it is."

"What?"

"You know I've been gathering all the information I can on Vandalay."

"Yeah."

"Well, I had the library send me every magazine and newspaper they could find in their archives about The Jungle." She took a deep breath. "Mitch I'm staring at a photo of Marcus Dellafield and Dick Vandalay with their arms around each other, posing for the camera. Circa 1977."

"So?"

"So this could be it."

He switched the phone to his other ear, wondering if he'd been working too much overtime. Because he didn't get her point.

"Don't you see?" she continued. "Vandalay traffics in imported aphrodisiacs. Products like powdered rhinoceros horns and seahorses and tiger genitals. Things you can only find in the most remote places. According to Dellafield's bio, he's been all over the world. Including the very places where he'd have access to these animals."

Mitch blinked. "But Dellafield passed away last year. He can't be Vandalay's supplier."

But Elaine wasn't so easily discouraged. "Maybe his daughter is taking over the business. This research project gives her the perfect cover. She can touch base with Vandalay and contact all the couriers."

He couldn't deny that some of the pieces fit. Especially when he remembered the intense reaction Claire had elicited in him last night. And not only him, but seemingly every other man in the place. Maybe she'd been using some kind of aphrodisiac herself. Sprinkling something into their drinks, or more likely, dousing herself in some kind of aphrodisiac-spiked perfume.

He shook his head, knowing that was crazy. "Vandalay wouldn't assign me to watch over her if that was the case. The last thing Dick wants is a witness to any of those illegal transactions."

"You're giving him too much credit. Not many

criminals are known for their brains," Elaine countered. "Besides, he thinks you're just a bouncer. He doesn't know you're looking for this stuff."

"I still say it's a long shot."

"At this point, it's the only one we've got. Get close to her, Mitch. Use some of that magical Malone charm. Before you know it, she'll be telling you all her deepest, darkest secrets."

He wasn't so sure. In the last twenty-four hours, he'd learned that Claire had an iron will. Along with an incredible body. He'd have to walk a fine line—earning her trust without taking their relationship too far. He'd already crossed the line last night.

"All right," he agreed at last, knowing he really didn't have any other choice. "I'll get close to her and see what I can find out."

"If I know you," Elaine said, amusement in her voice, "that shouldn't take long. Keep me posted."

"I will. Now you get back in bed." Mitch hung up, then clipped the cell phone onto his belt. He looked up the stairs and thought about what awaited him. A woman who might have the power to make him forget this was all just part of the job.

But he'd worry about that later.

CLAIRE HID A YAWN BEHIND her hand as she slipped off the bar stool and folded the last release form into her purse. It had been a long night, but a successful one. She had all ten male volunteers lined up for the research project. Now it was time to go back to the apartment and insert the data she'd collected into the computer.

But halfway to the door, she found her path blocked by a familiar broad chest. She arched her neck to look up into a pair of intense blue eyes. In that instant, the rhythm of her heart matched the beat of the dance music. She swallowed. "Hello, Mitch."

"I accept," he said without preamble.

"What?"

"Your offer to take me on as a research assistant. I've changed my mind."

Claire took a step back to give herself more breathing room. Maybe lack of oxygen explained the sudden inability of her brain to function. "What?"

One corner of Mitch's mouth kicked up in what could almost be called a smile. "You're repeating yourself."

She took a deep breath. "But I thought you made it perfectly clear that the last thing you want to do is help me with this project."

"A man can change his mind, can't he?"

Warning bells went off in her head. Claire usually wasn't the suspicious type, but something wasn't right. Maybe it was the tone of his voice. Or the way he was looking at her. Like the tigers in Borneo that paced the perimeters of the villages at dusk.

"Not a man like you," Claire replied at last. "Not without a good reason."

Mitch turned from her for a moment to card three young women who appeared in the doorway.

Women who looked plenty old enough to her. Was he stalling? Trying to come up with an answer that would satisfy her?

Over the loud music, she heard one of the women ask Mitch to dance. He politely refused, then turned to face Claire once again. "So when do we start?"

"You still haven't answered my question. What's with this sudden overwhelming desire to help me with the research project?"

His gaze flickered from her face, but not before she glimpsed an undefinable gleam in his eyes. "Maybe I don't want to be a bouncer all of my life. 'Research Assistant' might look good on my résumé."

"I see."

He folded his arms across his chest. "Besides, you need someone around to protect you if another mob forms."

She waved off his concern. "That won't happen."

"How can you be so sure?"

"Because I won't wear the skirt."

His gaze dropped to her beige leather skirt. "So you believe not wearing a skirt will make you *less* desirable to men?"

Desirable? Claire savored the little tingle the compliment gave her. Even though she knew his perception of her was artificially induced. But for some reason, she wasn't ready to share that fact with him. "You haven't even asked what the job entails."

"So tell me."

"You'll have to accompany me on all interviews.

Mr. Vandalay was adamant on that point. Perhaps I'll even have you conduct a few yourself. I'll need help gathering some background data on The Jungle."

"Anything else you'll want me to do?"

She cleared her throat. "We'll see what comes up."

His eyes glimmered. "Sounds good to me."

Claire suppressed a shiver at the innuendo in his voice. Maybe this wasn't such a great idea after all. "Before you accept my job offer, I think you should know that it means asking these men some very sensitive questions about their love lives. Their innermost feelings."

He couldn't quite hide his grimace.

"See," she said with a satisfied smile. "You will hate it."

"No," he countered, taking a deep breath. "Women keep telling me I need to learn to be more...sensitive." He spit out the word like it left a bad taste in his mouth. "To communicate more."

Claire's smile widened. Maybe this could be fun. She'd enjoy seeing Mitch Malone off balance for a change. "All right, you're hired."

"So when do we start?"

"How about tomorrow? We could meet for lunch and discuss the details."

He nodded. "Where do you want to meet?"

"How about my apartment?" she suggested. "Then I can show you the computer program I have set up for the study."

"Great. What's the address?"

"It's on the sixth floor of The Willoughby. Central Park West."

He whistled low. "Just how much do cultural anthropologists make?"

"It's a sublet," she told him, deciding to skip the part about the skirt. She kind of liked the fact that he thought she had started that bar brawl all on her own. "My roommates and I got a great deal."

"So what time do you want me to pick you up?"

"How about noon?"

He nodded. "I'll see you then."

Claire walked out of The Jungle, welcoming the tepid breeze on her flushed face. Mitch Malone was now, officially, her research assistant. This was it. The chance to take Petra up on her challenge to find some passion in life.

And she might consider doing just that—once this research project was complete.

7

THE NEXT DAY, MITCH found himself in the foyer of The Willoughby under interrogation by the doorman.

"You've never seen *The Wizard of Oz?*" Franco Rossi shook his head in stunned disbelief. "The munchkins? The flying monkeys? The Wicked Witch of the West?"

"That's right." Mitch tucked his hands in the front pockets of his jeans. "So I can't give you the password because I have no idea who played the good witch Glinda."

"Man, that is so easy." Franco shook his head. "It was Billie Burke!"

"Now that we have that settled, will you let me in the building?" He glanced at his watch. "Like I said before, Claire Dellafield is expecting me."

Franco held up his hands. "Let me lend you the videotape of *The Wizard of Oz*. Because you are culturally bankrupt, man. And I deeply believe in doing my part to help those less fortunate."

"If I've survived this long without seeing *The Wizard of Oz*, I think I can stand it for another day or two."

Franco began to argue with him, but the elevator doors opened and Claire stepped into the foyer. She held a leash with well-coiffed poodle on the other end. The poodle growled at Franco.

Franco growled back.

Claire looked up at Mitch. "There's been a slight change of plans."

"You've hired the dog as your research assistant?"

She smiled. "No such luck. Cleo has an appointment with her therapist and it's my turn to take her."

"Who is Cleo?" Mitch asked.

"That's her." Franco pointed at the dog. "Short for Cleopatra. And our Cleo definitely has some emotional problems. I think she should be committed."

The poodle bared her teeth at Franco and emitted a low growl from deep in her throat.

Franco backed up a step.

"I don't think she likes you," Mitch told him.

"The feeling is mutual. I don't know why my boyfriend allows Higgy to keep that mutt here. Especially when she extorts Tavish's summer tenants into becoming her unpaid dog walkers."

"Who is Higgy?" Mitch asked, feeling lost in this conversation.

"Mrs. Higgenbotham," Claire told him. "She owns Cleo and lives in the apartment next to the one I'm staying in this summer."

"There's definitely a family resemblance," Franco added, then screamed when he saw Cleo squat in the corner of the foyer. "Not again you nasty little French furball!" He crouched into a karate pose.

Claire bent down and swept the poodle into her

arms, then motioned for Mitch to follow her. "We'd better go. See you later, Franco."

"Ciao, Claire," he said, standing upright again. Then his gaze raked over her. "By the way, you look simply smashing in that sundress. Turquoise is definitely your color. Don't you think so, Mitch?"

Mitch had been trying not to notice. But now he had an excuse to let his eyes linger. The dress was held up on her shoulders by thin straps. The bodice revealed just enough of the curve of her cleavage to make him want to see more, then tapered to her slender waist before flaring into a full skirt. "Nice."

Franco tapped his chin as he studied Mitch. "Have you ever had your colors done?"

Mitch shook his head. "I don't think so. I don't even know what that means."

"I'd guess you're a winter," Franco continued, "although I can't be absolutely certain in this light. If you're free tonight, stop by Apartment 101 for a consultation. It belongs to my boyfriend, but he loves it when I invite guests over. We might even have time to watch *The Wizard of Oz*. Make a night of it."

"I'll keep that in mind," Mitch replied, following Claire out the door. She was laughing by the time they both reached the sidewalk.

"What's so funny?" he asked

"The look on your face." Claire gasped for air as Cleo sniffed the concrete in front of them. "Were you afraid Franco was asking you out on a date?"

"Absolutely not," Mitch replied. "He already has a boyfriend and Franco strikes me as the loyal type."

"He is," she agreed. "Especially to his tenants. Well, except for Mrs. Higgenbotham. For some reason, they don't get along very well."

"The fact that he's a little wacko might have something to do with it."

"I know he's a little eccentric, but he's also very nice. How many doormen in New York City offer free color consultations?"

"He's definitely one of a kind," Mitch replied as they headed down the sidewalk. "Although, I think Franco needs a therapist more than Cleo does. Did you see the way he was growling at the dog? And what was with that crazy kung fu move?"

"Franco has black belts in karate and judo. Plus he knows everything about everyone who lives in this place."

Mitch liked the way Claire's long ponytail bobbed behind her head as she walked. And the way her hips swayed just enough to capture a man's attention. Not that *he* was paying attention. "So does that mean I should go to Franco if I want to find out more about you?"

Her gaze met his. "Why the sudden interest in me?"

Good question. He lifted his shoulders in a noncommittal shrug. "You're my new boss. I'm just curious how tough you're going to be to work for."

She smiled. "According to my students, I'm the reincarnation of Attila the Hun. I teach cultural anthropology at Penleigh College in Indiana. But don't worry, Mitch, I won't grade your performance."

Then her face turned beet red. "Work performance," she sputtered. "I won't grade your work performance."

"Okay," he replied, slightly confused. Maybe it was time to change the subject. "Where exactly are we going?"

"Park Avenue. Cleo's therapist works out of his home there."

Mitch looked down at the dog. "So why does Cleo need to see a shrink anyway?"

Claire leaned toward him and said softly, "She's suffering from a severe case of CID. Otherwise known as canine intimacy dysfunction."

"Why are you whispering?"

She laughed. "I don't know. Probably because Mrs. Higgenbotham covered Cleo's ears when she explained her problems. Apparently, she's very sensitive."

"What exactly is canine intimacy dysfunction? Or do I want to know?"

"Probably not. But I'll tell you anyway," Claire said. They slowed down as they reached the intersection, waiting for the crosswalk signal to change. "In layman's terms, CID means Cleo's not interested in any of the studs that Mrs. Higgenbotham arranges for her."

"You're joking?"

Claire shook her head. "It's no joke to Mrs. Higgenbotham. Especially since she's had to pay exorbitant stud fees. And now one of the stud's owners is suing her."

"Suing a dog?"

She nodded. "Apparently, the stud doesn't take rejection well, so Cleo had to make her disinterest clear by biting him in a very sensitive place. It required ten stitches."

Mitch winced. "Ouch."

The light changed and they crossed the street with Cleo leading the way. Mitch's gaze slid to the woman walking beside him, astounded by their relatively cordial conversation. Astounded by her, period. He liked the way the sunlight cast golden glints in her hair. The contrast of her creamy skin against the sundress. The way her lips curved into a smile when she looked up at him.

"Cleo has another problem," Claire announced as they headed down another sidewalk.

Mitch thought about the incident in the apartment foyer. "Incontinence?"

"No." Claire motioned to the hot dog stand beside them. "An insatiable craving for hot dogs. She won't move until we buy her one."

He glanced down to the poodle looking woefully up at the hot dog stand. "This dog's only problem seems to be that she's spoiled."

He bent down to pick her up and carry her past the

stand, but Cleo snapped at his outstretched hands with her razor-sharp teeth.

Mitch drew back. "Or maybe just hungry. How about you, Claire? Can I buy you lunch? I guarantee you won't taste a hot dog this good in Indiana."

She nodded. "Thanks. I am hungry. Make mine with relish and mustard."

He turned to the vendor, pulling his wallet out of his back pocket. "Three hot dogs, please. One plain with no bun. Two with the works."

"Mitch," Claire protested, but he ignored her.

"Here we go," he said, handing her the hot dog, then breaking Cleo's plain one into small pieces before placing them on the sidewalk.

Claire adjusted the leash in her right hand as she tried to balance the hot dog in her left. "Why did you order the works? I hate sauerkraut and the onions are spilling out all over."

"Take a bite," he said, peeling back the wrapper on his own. "You'll love it."

She hesitated, then took a tentative bite, chewing thoughtfully. "Not bad."

"It's delicious," Mitch countered, grinning as Claire took a second bite. "Admit it."

"Okay," she agreed. "It's the best hot dog I've ever tasted. How is that possible?"

"This wonderful New York air gives it a special flavor all its own."

As she took another bite, a glob of ketchup and sauerkraut dropped out of the other end of the bun. It plopped onto her collarbone and began sliding down into the bodice of her dress.

"Oh no..." she cried, her hands too full to stop it.

Mitch reacted before he had time to think, slipping his fingers just inside the top of her dress to scoop out the sauerkraut.

Claire sucked in a deep, audible breath as he encountered silky soft skin in the crevice of her breasts and felt the rapid beat of her heart beneath his fingertips. The contact was over in an instant, but Mitch felt oddly disoriented.

He hastily stepped away from her as he wiped the mess off his fingers. Then he took the dog leash from her and handed her a clean napkin. "Here you go."

"Thanks," she said, not quite meeting his gaze as she daintily dabbed away the smear of ketchup on her skin.

Mitch's body hardened as he watched her trail the napkin down from her collarbone to the swell of her breast. He ached to do it himself, realizing that brief touch just made him want to touch her all the more.

Not a good idea. The thought of Elaine in that hospital bed cooled his blood. What the hell was he doing lusting after Claire when he had a job to do? Hadn't he already learned his lesson?

He forced himself to look away from her, then noticed the rest of her hot dog lying on the ground. Cleo pounced on it and gobbled it up in one gulp. "Here, let me buy you another one."

"That's really not necessary," Claire said, her cheeks burning. "I'm really not hungry."

He wished he could say the same. She'd missed a little dab of ketchup just above her left breast. For one fleeting, insane moment, he had the urge to lean forward and lick it off.

Not smart. Not if he wanted to solve this case. He hadn't even asked her anything about her father's connection to Vandalay yet. But he knew he had to take it slow. The last thing he wanted to do was arouse her suspicions.

Or arouse himself again. "So tell me more about this research study. How exactly does it work?"

Claire nudged a sated Cleo away from the hot dog stand and around the corner. "There are three phases. One is the observation phase, which basically consists of taking notes regarding the interactions between men and women at The Jungle."

"Why The Jungle?" he asked. "There are a lot of singles bars in New York City, most of them nicer than the one you picked."

"But that's just it," Claire replied. "I didn't pick it. Twenty-five years ago, The Jungle was the trendiest nightspot in the city. My father chose it to research how people interacted with strangers at the height of the sexual revolution. Now I want to see if anything has changed since then, with the patrons of The Jungle and with the nightclub itself."

Was that really all there was to it? Or had Elaine's

instincts been right? "So how does Dick Vandalay fit into all of this?"

"I'll definitely want to interview him. He was there in the beginning and can give me wonderful insights just by telling me about things he's seen."

Maybe that's how he could nail Vandalay. Suggest some questions that would catch the guy off guard. Questions that had left both Mitch and Elaine frustrated since the beginning of this investigation. There were no guarantees, of course, but anything was better than sitting in neutral.

"I'm free the rest of the afternoon if you want to interview him today."

Claire shook her head. "He's last on my list. I don't want his opinions to color the rest of my research."

Last on her list. That meant he'd have plenty of time to investigate Claire's possible involvement in this case. There was only one problem—she seemed totally committed to this project. Either she was a great actress or this research project wasn't simply a cover for trafficking in illegal substances.

"There it is." Claire pointed to the other side of the street.

"Are you sure?" Mitch looked at the well-appointed buildings lining Park Avenue.

She nodded. "That's the address Mrs. Higgenbotham gave me. And Cleo seems to recognize it."

Mitch glanced down to the poodle straining at the leash. "Cleo probably can't wait to diss all those

studs. Exactly how does she converse with her therapist, anyway?"

"I didn't ask."

"Smart girl."

When they reached the clinic, Claire turned the
poodle over to the receptionist while Mitch waited
out in the hallway.

"We're supposed to pick up Cleo in an hour,"
Claire told him as they walked out of the clinic. "Just
enough time to do one interview."

"With who?" he asked, hoping she'd changed her
mind about Vandalay.

She smiled up at him. "You."

8

"SHALL WE BEGIN?" CLAIRE asked, as they sat at a sidewalk café located just across the street from Dr. Fielding's office. Her notepad lay open on the black wrought-iron table and she clicked the mechanical pencil in her hand.

Mitch set down the grape soda she'd bought him. "Tell me again why we have to do this?"

"Because I want to work out any kinks in the questionnaire before I begin the interviews." That sounded good. Reasonable. She hoped he bought it.

"And?" he prodded, obviously not buying it. His perceptive blue gaze made her fidget in the wrought-iron chair. He was awfully inquisitive for a bouncer.

"And I'm a little nervous about asking strange men to tell me about their sex lives," she confided. "I thought if I could get through some of these more intimate questions with you, my subjects should be a breeze."

A smile hiked up one corner of Mitch's mouth. "Am I so terrifying?"

Yes. For all the wrong reasons. Terrifying because she'd rather throw her notepad aside and concentrate on him instead of the research project. Terrifying because she couldn't forget that kiss they'd shared. A kiss he'd probably already forgotten.

"Of course not. You're just..." Claire's voice faltered as she tried to think of a way to describe Mitch that wouldn't reveal her attraction to him.

And Mitch wasn't trying to help her out, either. He just sat sipping his grape soda and looking much too sexy for his own good. Or hers.

"You're the strong, silent type," she said at last. "They're harder to read."

He shrugged his broad shoulders. "Last I heard, women liked the strong, silent type."

"They might say they do," she countered. "But studies show that lack of communication is one of the major reasons couples seek counseling."

Mitch leaned forward, his muscles flexing beneath his short-sleeved cotton shirt. "So what kind of man do you prefer? Silent or chatty?"

Claire slid her gaze back up to his face. "This isn't about me. I need to remain an impartial observer in this study and not let the subjects turn the interview around on me. Like you're attempting to do right now. My personal likes and dislikes are immaterial."

"Not to me."

His words made her grip the pencil more tightly as she carefully printed his name at the top of the notepad. *What did that mean?*

"Question number one," she began, deciding to ignore his comment and forge ahead with the interview. "How many sexual encounters have you had in the last year...?"

"I don't mark notches on my bedpost," he said wryly.

"Less than ten?" Claire continued as though he hadn't interrupted her. "Ten to fifteen? Fifteen to twenty-five? Or more than twenty-five?"

"Define sexual encounter."

She lifted her gaze from the notepad. "You don't understand the question?"

He leaned forward. "Are you talking about actual sexual intercourse or any physical contact with a woman that I find pleasurable? Like when I carried you out of The Jungle the other night."

"Physical *sexual* contact," she clarified.

Mitch's voice grew husky. "Like carrying you out of The Jungle."

Heat rushed to Claire's cheeks. "Since we were both wearing clothes at the time, I certainly don't think that counts as sexual contact."

Mitch set his grape soda on the table. "So you believe a person has to be completely naked for a physical sexual encounter to occur?"

"Of course not," she sputtered. "But simple physical contact isn't the same as sex. Neither one of us had a craving for a cigarette after you threw me into that taxi. Which I did not find *pleasurable* at all!"

He grinned at her. "Gotcha."

She blinked. "What?"

"You're not supposed to let the subject turn the interview around on you, remember? Your personal feelings are immaterial. You failed the test, Claire. Want to try it again?"

She took a deep breath and resisted the urge to pour the rest of his grape soda in his lap. "Let's just continue the interview, shall we? I'm still waiting for you to answer the first question."

"Can you repeat it for me?"

"How many sexual encounters have you had in the last year. Less than ten. Ten to fifteen…"

He held up one hand. "I remember that part."

"You can be honest," she told him. "Don't worry about trying to impress me."

He thought about it for a moment, adding them up in his head. "Less than ten."

"That's all?" she asked, slightly skeptical.

"You don't believe me?"

"It's just that a man like you…"

He arched a brow, waiting for her to continue.

"Maybe we should move onto the next question."

He shook his head. "I want to hear why you don't believe me."

Claire met his gaze. "Maybe it has something to do with the way you kissed me last night. It certainly seemed like you've had a lot of practice."

Mitch grinned. "Thank you."

"Are you sure the answer is less than ten?"

"Why does it matter?" he asked. "This is just a practice interview."

He was right. She jotted down his answer.

Mitch leaned closer. "So how many sexual encounters have you had, Claire?"

But she wasn't about to let him trap her into reversing the interview again. Or to reveal any details about her almost nonexistent sex life. "Let's move on to question two now."

He leaned back in his chair, taking his grape soda with him. "Okay."

"On average, how long do your relationships with women last? Your choices are—less than one month, one month to three months, three to six months, or six months or longer."

"Less than a month."

She looked up at him. "So you're not seeking a long-term relationship?"

"Is that a question?"

"More like a deduction." She jotted a note to herself in the margin. "Although I suppose I should ask a follow-up question. Who usually initiates the breakup? You or the woman you're involved with?"

"It's usually mutual." Mitch tipped up the soda can and drained it. "And usually caused by the fact that she was attracted to the strong, silent type, then suddenly decides she wants to start communicating. It always goes downhill from there."

Claire couldn't help but smile at the bewilderment she heard in his voice. "Question number three— name the physical features that attract you to a woman."

"I've never broken it down before," Mitch said,

studying her. "I like a woman with nice eyes. A nice smile. Nice breasts."

"Does that mean big breasts?" Claire asked, her pen poised over the paper. Her curiosity was strictly professional.

"No, it means..." He sighed, "I don't know what the hell it means. I just know what I like."

"It would really help me if you could be more specific."

"You want an example?"

"If that would make it easier for you to answer the question."

"Okay, take your breasts for instance." His gaze dropped below her neck. "They're nice. Not too big. Not too small. Nice."

Claire arched a brow at him. "Is this another attempt to draw me into the interview?"

"No," he said honestly. "It's an attempt to answer the question. But if we start talking about the size of my...physical attributes, I'm outta here."

She bit back a smile, sorely tempted to do just that. But she didn't want him to leave just yet. Not when she still had fifteen more questions left on her form. "Question number four..."

MITCH WANTED BONUS PAY. Revealing his private love life to a nubile professor had not been covered in his law enforcement training. How the hell was he supposed to keep his mind on the job when she kept asking him about sex?

He answered the remainder of her questions as truthfully as possible, all too aware of her breasts since she'd brought up the subject. Or had he? Mitch didn't remember anymore. He was too busy trying not to stare at them.

This had to stop. He'd taken a vow to stay celibate until this case was solved and he damn well intended to keep it. Fantasizing about Claire was only going to make his job that much harder. Along with certain parts of his anatomy.

He shifted in his chair, telling himself this must be some kind of test. If he failed, he'd bungle the case and let down Elaine—again. If he passed, he'd solve the case and could put his guilt about Elaine's accident behind him once and for all. Nothing could be simpler.

So why couldn't he stop thinking about what Claire looked like naked?

An eternity later, Claire finally closed the notepad with a satisfied sigh. "I think that went fairly well, considering it was my first time." Then she glanced at her watch. "Speaking of time, I need to pick up Cleo."

Mitch breathed a silent sigh of relief as he got up out of his chair. The humidity had risen steadily all afternoon and a sheen of perspiration shone on Claire's forehead. Small strands of hair had come loose from her ponytail and now lay in damp curls on her cheeks and forehead.

"I'll come with you," he said, though what he really wanted to do was go home and take a cold shower. Or three.

"That isn't necessary," she said, stuffing the note-pad into her bulging tote bag, then swinging it over her shoulder. "I'm sure it's out of your way."

"You mentioned inputting data into your computer." He pushed in his chair. "I thought I should see the setup in case I have any questions." Thanks to that goofy doorman, he hadn't even been able to see her apartment when he'd arrived to pick her up.

Claire hesitated. "Actually, I'm taking the long way home. Cleo is supposed to walk in Central Park after her therapy sessions to release nervous energy."

"After that interview, I'm feeling a little nervous energy myself. A walk in the park sounds great." So did a dip in a fountain. Then maybe he could keep his mind on his job instead of Claire's breasts.

The poodle wasn't quite ready when they walked into the Dr. Fielding's office. Mitch followed Claire into the crowded reception room, amazed at the number of people in New York City who believed in dog therapy. And actually paid for it.

The receptionist hailed them from her desk. "Dr. Fielding would like to speak to you for a moment. His consultation room is the second door on the left."

Claire glanced over her shoulder at Mitch, then motioned for him to come with her. Canned classical music drifted from the wall speakers and the hallway was filled with framed photographs of smiling dogs.

At least, they looked happy. No doubt the result of intensive canine therapy.

The consultation door was open and the doctor stood up as they entered. He rounded his massive mahogany desk and held out one beefy hand. "You must be Cleo's parents. She's told me so much about you. I'm Dr. Fielding."

"Cleo talks to you?" Mitch interjected, unable to help himself.

"Nonverbally, of course," Dr. Fielding said with a hearty chuckle. "But sometimes that can be even more powerful than words." He turned to Claire. "Don't you agree, Mrs. Higgenbotham?"

"Actually, I'm Cleo's neighbor," she informed him, reaching out to shake his hand. "Claire Dellafield. And this is Mitch Malone."

"Well," the doctor said with a sigh, perching himself on the corner of his desk, "this is delightful. I'm always happy to see community support for my patients. That is so important in their recovery."

"Where is Cleo?" Claire asked, looking around the spacious office.

"She's having her manicure," Dr. Fielding replied. "It's a standard part of our treatment program."

"Is there a reason you wanted to see us?" Claire asked. "It might be better if you spoke directly with Mrs. Higgenbotham."

"No, no," he assured her. "You can just pass my message on to her, if you will. I just wanted to assure everyone who cares about Cleo's welfare that the session went very well today. I think with continued intensive therapy, Cleo will successfully overcome her fear of intimacy."

"Just curious," Mitch intoned. "But how much do you charge for a session?"

"The standard," he replied. "Two-fifty an hour."

"Two *hundred* and fifty dollars?" Mitch asked.

"That's right," Dr. Fielding replied cheerfully. "Naturally, that includes the manicure, the biofeedback session and the past life regression therapy."

"Naturally," Mitch said, then muttered. "I'm in the wrong business."

The door opened and a young woman in a white lab coat walked in carrying Cleo in her arms. "This little sweetheart is all ready to go, Doctor."

"Wonderful." Dr. Fielding picked Cleo up in his big hands and held her up in the air. "Hello, my little snookums. Aren't you a beauty? So dainty. So precious."

Cleo growled at him.

Dr. Fielding handed the poodle to Mitch. "Positive feedback. Vital to recovery."

Mitch handed the poodle to Claire, not so sure it was the dog who needed the therapy. "I'll keep that in mind."

Claire held Cleo in her arms. "All we need is her leash and we'll be ready to go."

A spasm of horror crossed the doctor's face. "That is not a good idea. Leashes, or restrictions of any kind, are very detrimental to the kind of therapy I practice."

"They just happen to be the law in this city," Mitch reminded him.

Dr. Fielding sighed. "True. But I must insist that you exert no pressure on the leash unless absolutely necessary to ensure her safety. Let Cleo lead the way. Give her a sense of freedom."

"Do you have the leash?" Claire asked.

The doctor rounded his desk and pulled open the drawer. He hesitated a moment before handing it to her. "Please use it with utmost care."

"I'll do my best," she assured him.

It took them ten minutes to get out of the building since the poodle was leading the way. Cleo stopped to sniff every plant, investigate every corner, and bark incessantly at every other canine patient bigger than she was.

"It could take a while to get to Central Park at this rate," Claire said, holding the leash loosely in her hand. But Cleo's ears picked up at the mention of the park and she turned on the sidewalk and began trotting in that direction.

By the time they reached Central Park, both Mitch and Claire were half jogging to keep up with the dog.

"Finally," Claire huffed, slumping onto a park bench as the poodle rolled in the lush grass.

Mitch sat down beside her. "Tired?"

"Just a little," she replied, trying not to gasp for air.

Mitch wasn't even breathing hard. "Do you think Cleo's regained her sense of freedom yet?"

But before Mitch could answer, Cleo sat up at the sound of a pigeon rooting around in the bushes beside them. Cleo lunged for it, ripping the leash out of Claire's palm.

"I think she's definitely enjoying her freedom," Mitch said wryly.

Claire jumped to her feet. "Cleo, come back here! Right now!"

But the poodle was gone.

9

"DO YOU SEE HER ANYWHERE?" Claire turned in a slow circle under a large oak tree, looking for some sign of the poodle. She and Mitch had been fruitlessly searching Central Park for the last twenty minutes.

Mitch walked up beside her, raking his dark hair back off his forehead. "No. I can't believe she could disappear so quickly. That's the last time I listen to the advice of a dog therapist."

"I'll probably have to put up posters with Cleo's picture on them and offer a reward." She thought of the massive portrait of Mrs. Higgenbotham and her dog that hung above the stone fireplace in the Higgenbotham apartment. "Mrs. H is going to kill me. She might even kick us out of the apartment for this."

"Don't panic yet," Mitch told her. "That dog's got to be around here somewhere."

"How big is Central Park?"

"I'm not sure," he mused. "I think I read once that it's about eight hundred acres. Maybe a little more."

Claire groaned. "We can never cover that much ground in one day. What if Cleo is hurt? What if she falls into a pond? Or gets into a fight with another dog?"

"I'm sure Cleo knows how to dog-paddle. And from what you told me about that stud dog she almost ripped in two, she knows how to hold her own in any fight."

Claire plucked at the bodice of her sundress as perspiration trickled between her breasts. "So what should we do now? Call the police?"

Mitch's gaze moved from her chest to her face. "The police don't even start looking for a missing person until at least twenty-four hours have passed. Dogs aren't in their jurisdiction."

"So where do we go from here?"

"How about a hot dog stand? Maybe we can lure her out with a snack."

"Good idea." Claire moved off the sidewalk as a family of bicyclists sped by them. "Why don't we split up? You can go buy a hot dog while I keep searching for her."

He frowned. "I'm not sure that's such a good idea. I think we should stick together."

"But if we split up we can cover more ground." Claire pointed to the dense area of bushes behind them. "Cleo's probably chasing birds somewhere in there. If I can't get her to come out, maybe a hot dog will."

He surveyed the area, then gave a brisk nod and headed off in the opposite direction, turning to call out to her. "I'll be back in few minutes to help you search."

"Keep your eyes open for her," she called after him,

but she was quickly beginning to lose hope. Claire kept picturing how hysterical Mrs. Higgenbotham would be if she returned to the apartment minus one poodle. Franco would be happy, but she and her roommates might find themselves out on the street.

Besides, a pampered dog like Cleo certainly wouldn't know how to fend for herself in the wilderness. And to a dog used to living in a high-rise apartment, Central Park was about as wild as it got.

"Here, Cleo," Claire called coaxingly, walking down the path. "Come here, girl."

Claire moved into the taller brush area, looking for some sign of white and pink among all the greenery surrounding her. She pushed branches aside, wondering if that long leash might be caught on a branch somewhere. Maybe Cleo was trapped and couldn't come back to them.

Pigeons pecked at the ground and the damp soil began to cling to Claire's sandals as she moved farther into the bushes. A sound made her stop. It was a low growl. Cleo? She got down gingerly on her hands and knees and peered under the thick hedgerow.

Her palms sunk into the soft earth as she inhaled the musty scent of dead leaves. Her left knee scraped against a small stone as she crawled even farther under the bush. "Cleo? Cleopatra Higgenbotham, it's time to come out now."

But no poodle appeared. Claire began to scoot back out from the hedgerow when the sound of a low, snide voice made her freeze.

"Nice view."

The strange voice sent a chill down Claire's spine. She started to stand up until something cold and hard dug into the base of her spine. A gun?

"Drop back on your hands and knees," the man rasped. "Now."

She dropped back on the ground, too stunned for a moment to think straight.

"Now keep your eyes straight ahead," he ordered. "And give me the bag."

Claire's heart pounded triple time as she slid the tote bag off her shoulder. This couldn't be happening. She was actually being mugged. In Central Park. Her fingers shook as she tossed the tote bag behind her. It contained a small amount of cash, her apartment key and the notes she'd taken at the practice interview today. Detailed notes about Mitch's sex life.

"Can I keep the notepad?" she asked, irritated to hear her voice trembling.

"There ain't shit in here," the mugger exclaimed as he upended the tote bag and dumped the contents on the ground beside her. "What else you got?"

She closed her right fist in attempt to hide the emerald ring her father had given her on their first anthropological study together in Colombia ten years ago. It was a small, rare trapiche emerald and quite valuable. But the furtive movement must have caught the mugger's attention.

"Hand the ring over."

"No," she blurted. But the gun dug deeper into her

spine and she knew it would be stupid to give her life for a ring. No matter how much it meant to her.

Biting down hard on her lower lip, she tugged the ring off her finger. It finally slipped over her knuckle and she pressed it hard into her palm before finally holding her arm back toward him.

The mugger jerked the ring out of her hand. "A little puny, but not bad."

A movement in the bushes in front of her made Claire look up. Mitch was there under the hedgerow, several feet away, also on his hands and knees, searching for Cleo. She had to find a way to warn him before he made his presence known to the mugger.

"So how big is that gun?" she asked loudly.

Mitch looked up at her, confusion on his face.

"Big enough to blow you to pieces," the mugger replied with a low chuckle.

Mitch's eyes narrowed as he surveyed the scene in front of him. She saw his jaw clench as he angled his body to get a better view of the man holding her at gunpoint. He began to slowly back out of the bushes, ignoring her frantic silent pleas to stay put.

Claire closed her eyes, fearing the worst. Not only had she lost Cleo, but now Mitch's life was in danger. She might even lose him. Permanently.

"I think you'd better go now," Claire told the mugger. "Someone might see you."

"Got any more jewelry on ya?" he asked, ignoring her advice. Then he shuffled closer and she could smell stale tobacco and pepperoni on his fetid breath. "Maybe I'll just have a little look-see for myself."

Claire tensed, ready to make a run for it when she heard the man grunt behind her. Followed by the loud crunch of bone connecting with bone. She glanced over her shoulder to see the mugger lying on the ground, with Mitch hovering over him, his fists clenched.

"Be careful," she shouted, scrambling to her feet. "He's got a gun!"

But the only thing the mugger reached for was his nose, which was now bleeding profusely and looked slightly off-kilter.

Mitch bent down and picked up something off the ground. "It's not a gun. It a stick of pepperoni."

Claire's jaw dropped as she stared at his hand. Her assailant's weapon was a one-inch round tube of processed meat you could pick up in any deli. She whirled on the mugger. "Pepperoni? You mugged me with pepperoni?"

"My nose," the mugger wailed beneath the hands covering his bloody face. "I think he broke my nose."

Anger welled up inside of her. She bent down and rifled through the mugger's coat pockets until she found her ring. Then she grabbed the pepperoni out of Mitch's hand and whacked it hard against the mugger's knee. It broke in half and she tossed it aside in frustration.

A white poodle scampered out from underneath the hedge and pounced on it.

"Cleo!" Claire exclaimed. Then for no good reason at all, she burst into tears.

Mitch grabbed the end of Cleo's leash and secured it around a tree branch. Then he pulled Claire into his arms, his hand gently clasping the back of her head as he murmured words of comfort into her ear.

She didn't comprehend what he said and it didn't matter. Just the feel of him soothed her; he was big, strong, solid. She burrowed into the safe cocoon of his arms and let the trembles fade from her body.

When she pulled back at last, she glimpsed the empty ground behind him. "The mugger's gone."

Mitch glanced over his shoulder, then turned back to her. "That's okay. I don't think he'll be assaulting anyone with a pepperoni for a while."

"I hope that broken nose taught him a lesson," Claire said, anger welling within her once more. She fingered the emerald ring on her hand, realizing how close she'd come to losing it forever.

"He's lucky he doesn't have a broken kneecap," Mitch teased. "The way you whacked him with that pepperoni, you might have even left a bruise."

"You're making jokes," she said, hiccuping now as her tears subsided.

"Yeah," he drawled softly. "I do that when I'm scared out of my mind."

She looked up into his blue eyes, touched by the concern she saw there. "What else do you do?"

"This." Then he lowered his head and kissed her. Not like the kiss outside The Jungle. That had been hot and deep and primal. This kiss was like a gentle rain on her lips. Soothing. Renewing. Almost reverent.

Claire placed her hands on his chest, feeling the steady beat of his heart under her fingertips.

Mitch pulled back, breaking the kiss almost as soon as it had started. Then he brushed a lone tear off one of her cheeks with the pad of his thumb.

Claire took a deep breath and stepped away from him, trying not to read too much into that kiss. But her heart skipped a beat all the same.

"Sorry," he said abruptly.

"No, I'm sorry," she replied, feeling a little giddy now. "I don't know what came over me. I hardly ever cry. It's just that I've never been mugged before."

He raked a hand through his hair. "I've never kissed a woman in Central Park before. Guess I shouldn't have taken advantage of you like that."

Claire winced as she turned to untie Cleo's leash, wondering if that meant he regretted that wonderful kiss already. "No problem. I'm just glad I got my ring back. And we found Cleo."

He bent down to gather the papers that had spilled out of her tote bag. "Thanks to that pepperoni."

She looked up at him, then burst out laughing. "I can't believe I thought it was a gun. I'm such an idiot."

"You did the right thing," he assured her. "Never take chances in a situation like that."

She planted her hands on hips. "You might try taking your own advice, Mr. Malone. You didn't know that was a pepperoni in his hand, either, when you went after him. You're a bouncer, Mitch, not a cop. If that guy had been holding a gun, he could have killed you!"

Mitch didn't say anything for a long moment, just stared at her as if he wanted to say something more. Then his gaze flickered as he shrugged his shoulders. "You're probably right."

"I know I'm right." They started walking along the path, Claire holding tightly to Cleo's leash this time. "Do you think we should go to the police?"

He shook his head. "They'll never find that guy now. Too many muggings happen every day for the police to investigate them all. But you can go ahead and give them a call if it will make you feel better."

She glanced down at the dirt clinging to her knees. "Right now the only thing I want to do is go home and take a long, hot bath."

"Looks like Cleo could use one, too," Mitch said, nodding toward the dog.

For the first time, Claire noticed the leafy debris clinging to the poodle's fur. She bent down to brush it out, but there were too many bits of leaves and grass stuck in too many hard to reach places.

"Don't worry about it," Mitch told her by the time they reached The Willoughby. "If Mrs. Higgenbotham is upset about the way Cleo looks, she can take the dog out herself next time."

"You're absolutely right." Claire brushed wet

leaves off her hands. "Do you mind looking at the computer setup another time? I really need to clean up."

"No problem," he replied, as they stood awkwardly on the sidewalk. The music from Franco's boom box in the foyer reverberated against the glass door. Franco was inside practicing shadow karate, too busy watching his reflection on the wall to notice them.

For some ridiculous reason, Claire felt like they were on a date and found herself wondering if he was going to kiss her again.

"Well, I guess I'll see you later," Mitch said at last. "When is the first interview?"

"On Thursday at two o'clock," she replied, realizing it would be three long days before she saw him again. "Does that work for you?"

He thought about it for a moment, then nodded. "Do you want me to pick you up?"

Claire shook her head. "It's in midtown, so there's no need for you to come all the way down here. Why don't we just meet up at the corner of Thirty-second and Broadway. Say around one forty-five?"

"Sounds good."

She smiled. "It will probably seem boring after today's excitement."

One corner of his mouth hitched up. "If there's one thing I've learned recently, it's that life around you is never boring."

Claire's life hadn't been boring since the day she'd

stepped into that black skirt. But how long would the magic last? "Well, goodbye."

"Bye."

Claire turned and walked Cleo into the building, resisting the urge to see if Mitch was watching her or if he'd already walked away. Franco turned as they walked through the door and Cleo lunged at him with a ferocious growl.

Franco waved his hand in front of his face. "Wow, talk about serious doggie breath. Did you feed the mutt pepperoni pizza for lunch?"

"It's a long story," Claire replied, then glanced briefly out the door. But the sidewalk was empty.

She wished she could say the same of her heart. So much had changed this afternoon. In those few fleeting moments before she discovered the mugger posed no real threat, she realized she didn't want to die with regrets. The regret of not pursuing passion. Both in her career and in her personal life.

Now she just had to figure out what to do about it.

When she delivered Cleo to Mrs. Higgenbotham, the woman was so appalled at the condition of the poodle's fur that Claire decided not to say anything about the incident in the park. But Dr. Fielding's positive report did seem to mollify the older woman a bit. She even thanked Claire before closing the door.

Claire stood in the hallway, knowing it was time to acknowledge her feelings. Walking down the hallway, she knocked on Petra's door before she had a chance to chicken out.

Petra smiled when she saw Claire standing there. "Claire! What a wonderful surprise."

She took a deep breath. "Tell me the best way to seduce a man."

10

"THAT'S SIMPLE," PETRA said, pulling Claire inside the apartment and closing the door behind her. "Find an excuse for one or both of you to get naked."

"Simple?" Claire plopped down on the loveseat. "Maybe for you. But not all of us sculpt naked men for a living."

An alabaster sculpture of a male torso was displayed on the glass-topped coffee table in front of her. All of Petra's sculptures captured a man's nude body from the neck to just above the knees. Claire had to admit it was both interesting and educational to see the vast proportional options available. It would be even more interesting to see how Mitch measured up.

"True," Petra mused, then grinned. "Why do you think I chose this career?" She motioned to the impressive collection of torsos scattered around the living room. "If any of these appeal to you, just let me know. I can give you his name and number."

Claire shook her head. "I'm not interested in just any man."

"Then who?"

She swallowed. "Mitch Malone."

"Ah." Petra smiled. "So I take it you went back into The Jungle."

Claire nodded. "It's a long story, but Mitch is working as my research assistant now." Then another thought occurred to her. "Wait a minute, I can't seduce him! That's sexual harassment."

Petra rolled her eyes. "This is the man who carried you bodily out of The Jungle, remember? Then he kissed you. I don't think he'll feel harassed if you simply let him know you're interested."

"But how exactly do I do that?" Claire asked. "Other than taking my clothes off."

Petra sat down opposite her. "What about that intriguing black skirt? It certainly sounds as if it did the job the last time you wore it."

Claire shook her head. "I really don't want to use any artificial means this time. It doesn't seem quite fair. Besides, I want Mitch to want me for me."

"Then you'll need to come up with a good strategy," Petra said simply. "Figure out his weak spots. What do you know about the man so far?"

"He's a great kisser," she began, remembering that interlude in the park. "Strong. Protective. Funny. But do I dare get involved with a man who claims that talking usually ruins his relationships?"

Petra arched a brow. "I didn't realize you were interested in talking."

Claire sagged back in the chair. "I can't believe we're even having this conversation."

Petra laughed. "Well, didn't you come to New

York City for the express purpose of studying human mating behavior? I think this is the perfect opportunity to put some of that research to good use."

"I did read a great article about using body language to send subliminal sexual messages. Maybe I could give that a try," Claire offered.

"I suppose that might work," Petra said thoughtfully. "If you prefer the more indirect approach. I still like the naked approach."

"Maybe this is a big mistake." Claire said, beset by more doubts. It was as if that kiss today had turned her brain to creamed corn. "What if a relationship with Mitch interferes with my work?"

"I believe ignoring your feelings for the man will be more detrimental to your work than acting on them. You can't put a lid on passion, Claire. It's bound to boil over eventually—and usually at the worst possible time."

Claire knew she couldn't be the only one feeling this spark between them. Not when Mitch had kissed her. Twice. The first time, she could blame the skirt. But today—that had been all on his own.

She stood up. "Thanks, Petra. I need to think about this a little more. But I appreciate the advice."

"You're welcome. Just be careful," her godmother warned. "If he breaks your heart, I'll have to kill him. And somehow I doubt the prison guards will model for me."

"I'll try to keep that in mind."

Claire just hoped it wasn't already too late.

ON THURSDAY AFTERNOON, Mitch stood on a corner in midtown Manhattan, waiting for Claire to show up for the first interview. She was already ten minutes late. His eyes scanned the street for some sign of her. Hopefully, she'd leave the poodle behind this time. For a poodle suffering from a case of canine intimacy dysfunction, that Cleo was a hell of a matchmaker.

Exactly what he *didn't* need in his life. Mitch had to stop kissing Claire. Now. Today. From this moment on, he'd deal with her in a strictly professional manner. Which meant no kissing, no mentally undressing her, no sexual fantasies. None. Zero. Zilch.

He turned to look down Thirty-second Street, expecting to see a familiar brunette among the crowd of commuters parading down the sidewalk. Ever since that kiss in Central Park, he'd been looking forward to seeing her again.

And that bothered him.

A taxicab pulled up to the curb and he saw Claire sitting in the back seat. His heart gave a strange little leap as she opened the door and stepped out.

"Stop it," he muttered to himself.

"Sorry, I'm late," Claire said with a smile. "Franco wanted to show me his latest karate move."

He found himself smiling back. "No problem."

"Actually, we do have a problem. Although, it's more of a good news, bad news situation."

"Give me the bad news first."

"Albert Ramirez had to postpone our interview. I

would have called to tell you, but I don't have your cell phone number."

"I don't like to give it out," he replied a moment before his cell phone rang.

Her smile widened. "Great timing."

"It's one of my many talents." Mitch pulled the phone off his belt to answer it. The voice on the other end made him swallow a groan. "Okay, I'll be there as soon as I can."

Claire's smile faded as she looked up at him. "You have to go somewhere?"

"Mrs. Cudahy is in crisis."

"Who's Mrs. Cudahy?"

"The lady who lives across the hall from me. She's a widow and her only son lives in Florida. She's moving down there in a few weeks. But in the meantime, the building superintendent refuses to answer any more of her calls."

"So she turns to you?"

"She's just a lonely old woman," Mitch explained, knowing he probably sounded like a pushover. But Mrs. Cudahy reminded him a little of the grandmother who had taken him in after his parents had abandoned him. Healing his pain with equal measures of oatmeal cookies and warm hugs.

"You'd better go then."

He hated the disappointment he heard in her voice. "Tell me your good news first."

"It's nothing important," she assured him. "After Mr. Ramirez bailed out on us, I was able to schedule an interview with another subject. I'm supposed to meet him at the Umbrella Café in an hour."

He folded his arms across his chest. "You're not going without me."

"You've already got a date with Mrs. Cudahy."

"The Umbrella is just a couple blocks from my place," Mitch told her. "Why don't you come with me? I can take care of Mrs. Cudahy's problem, then we can head over to the café for the interview."

Claire brightened at the suggestion and his heart inexplicably swelled in his chest. Or maybe it was just indigestion.

"Are you sure you don't mind if I tag along?" she asked as he hailed a taxi.

"You'll be doing me a favor."

"In what way?" Claire stood so close to the street that he held his arm out in front of her to shield her from the rush of traffic.

"Mrs. Cudahy keeps trying to marry me off to her niece," he said.

She smiled. "Really?"

He nodded. "I think she wants to make me part of the family before she moves to Florida. Maybe if she sees me with another woman, she'll get the hint that I'm not interested in matrimony."

"I'll do my best," Claire promised as a cab screeched to stop in front of them.

Ten minutes later, they were in Mitch's apartment building, riding the elevator to the third floor.

"This is nice," she said, as they stepped out into the

hallway. The odor of new carpet and fresh paint permeated the air.

It suddenly occurred to Mitch that a bouncer probably wouldn't be able to afford a place like this. Not that a cop's salary was anything to brag about, either, but still. He wanted to kick himself for his impulsive decision to invite her here. He mentally scanned his apartment in his mind, hoping there was nothing there that would give away his real occupation.

Mrs. Cudahy's door opened before they even reached it. "Oh, Mitch, I'm so glad you came. I didn't know what else to do. The bathtub is clogged again."

"I'm happy to help, Mrs. Cudahay." Then he turned to Claire. "This is a friend of mine, Claire Dellafield."

The older woman's eyes widened behind her bifocals. "How nice to meet you, Claire. Are you and Mitch...together?"

"I think he's very special," Claire said, sliding her hand into his. She squeezed gently and a jolt of electricity shot up his arm.

Mrs. Cudahy's face crinkled into a warm smile. "Well, isn't that nice. There nothing I like to see better than two people in love."

"He's told me a lot about you," Claire said, moving so close to him that his body went into high alert. She turned slightly toward him, one breast brushing against his arm. "Haven't you, Mitch?"

He swallowed hard. "Yeah."

The mischievous gleam in her eyes told she was relishing this opportunity to throw him off balance. No doubt she considered this payback for the times he'd done the same to her.

Mrs. Cudahy opened her door wider and waved them in. "There's no reason for you two to stand out in the hall. Come on in. I've got some cake already cut and I made a pitcher of iced tea."

"What about the drain?"

Mrs. Cudahy looked puzzled for a moment, then her face cleared. "Oh, yes. Do you mind taking a look at it for me? If it's not too much trouble."

"Not at all." Mitch walked toward the bathroom, very familiar with the layout of Mrs. Cudahy's apartment. The women's voices carried down the hallway, though he couldn't quite make out the words. Were they talking about him?

Five minutes later, he headed back toward the kitchen, wiping his hands on a towel.

"Were you able to fix it?" Mrs. Cudahy asked as she poured three glasses of iced tea.

"The drain is clear now," he told her, tossing the towel on the counter. "I found a sponge stuffed down in it."

"Well, isn't that strange," Mrs. Cudahy said, her round cheeks turning a bright pink. "I wonder how that could have happened?"

Then she pulled out a chair and motioned for Mitch to sit down next to Claire. "Now have some cake. It's German chocolate—your favorite kind. I'll dish up ice cream for us, too. And I packed some cookies for you to take home with you."

"You shouldn't go to so much trouble, Mrs. Cudahy," Mitch said, as he sat down.

"Oh, you're never any trouble," Mrs. Cudahy assured him as she walked over to the freezer.

Mitch picked up his fork, aware of Claire's eyes on him. He looked up and met her gaze. "What?"

"You're a pushover," she said softly, a note of surprise in her voice. "And a nice guy."

He leaned forward so only Claire could hear him. "This from a woman who takes her neighbor's dog to a therapist."

"It's in the contract," she countered.

"Right."

"Now, what are you two whispering about?" Mrs. Cudahy asked, setting a bowl heaped with vanilla ice cream in front of Mitch.

A challenge gleamed in Claire's eyes. "I was just telling Mitch that he shouldn't kiss me in front of you."

"Now you go right ahead. I was in love once, too, you know." Mrs. Cudahy placed one hand over her eyes. "I won't even look."

Mitch stared at his lovely anthropologist, knowing it would serve her right if he took her up on her dare. Maybe it was time to throw *her* off balance.

"Well, what are you waiting for?" Mrs. Cudahy asked, peeking through her fingers.

Claire daintily offered her cheek to him. But Mitch

grabbed the legs of her chair and jerked it next to him. Then he leaned forward and captured her mouth with his own.

He swallowed her tiny gasp of surprise, then lost himself in the taste of her. A wonderful combination of chocolate and Claire.

At last he pulled back, realizing he'd let that kiss go on much too long.

Claire blinked up at him with her big brown eyes, her lips pink and slightly swollen. "Wow."

"You can say that again," Mrs. Cudahy chuckled, pulling a chair up to the table. "You'd better grab him while you've got the chance, young lady. He's handy around the house, affectionate and he keeps a picture of his grandmother up in his apartment. What more could a girl want?"

Mitch took a deep breath, realizing he'd broken his own rule. He'd just kissed her. Again. This had to stop. From this moment on, he wouldn't think about kissing her again. Or about sex. Nothing. Zilch. Nada. No more kissing. No more touching. No more glances below the neck. He was a professional. It was time to start acting like one.

Mitch picked up his fork and turned his attention back to his cake. Bringing Claire here had been a big mistake. "I already told you, I'm not the marrying kind, Mrs. Cudahy."

"That's what they all say." Mrs. Cudahy winked at Claire. "Until they find the right girl."

Claire smiled at him and for a fleeting moment he

wondered if he had. Then he remembered she was still a suspect in the Vandalay case. A case he still hadn't come close to solving yet. Time to push the investigation into high gear. For Elaine. For his sanity.

From now on, the only interest Mitch had in Claire Dellafield was determining her involvement, or lack of it, in this case. Then he could move on.

Before he forgot that he wasn't the marrying kind.

11

TWO WEEKS LATER, MITCH stood just outside the door of the Ramirez brownstone. A light drizzle of rain fell from the cloudy sky and he leaned under the eaves as he punched Elaine's number into his cell phone.

She answered on the first ring. "Hello."

"It's Mitch. I just got your message." A burst of static crackled over the line.

"You'll never guess what I found out."

"How's the hip?" he interjected, feeling guilty for not visiting her more often. Between his bouncer duties at The Jungle, assisting Claire with this research project, and helping Mrs. Cudahy pack for her move, he barely had a spare moment to himself.

"Getting better every day."

"Good," he said, hoping like hell she was right. "So what's up?"

"I dug up some information on Professor Claire Dellafield."

His fingers tensed on the phone. "What kind of information?"

"She's got quite the travel résumé. South America, the Far East, New Zealand, Antigua. And that's just off the top of my head."

"So?"

"So these are the same places you'll find some of those aphrodisiacs we've traced to The Jungle."

"But I haven't turned up any evidence to connect Claire to this case yet." Fat raindrops began to fall from the sky, splattering his back.

Mitch had subtly interrogated Claire these last two weeks, asking about her father and her work. Listening to stories of the trips she'd taken as a child. Learning so many things about her. Like the fact that she shared his habit of indulging in movie marathons on the weekends. How she'd graduated from high school at sixteen and earned her master's degree at twenty-two. And he'd done it all without kissing her again.

That in itself was a miracle.

Especially since he'd had so many opportunities. Mrs. Cudahy had invited them to dinner on three separate occasions. Claire continued to excel in playing the part of his girlfriend. She was so good at it in fact, that he'd taken several cold showers in the last couple of weeks.

"There's got to be something there," Elaine insisted. "Claire Dellafield has had plenty of opportunity to make connections with people who traffic in illegal aphrodisiacs. And don't you find it a little odd that someone with her kind of connections is supposedly doing a research study at The Jungle?"

"Coincidence."

Elaine exhaled into the phone. "Maybe. All I'm saying is, keep your eyes open. Vandalay is still our main suspect, but we know he can't be working alone in this operation. Claire may be his supplier, or she may be simply lining him up with the right people."

"Claire's not involved."

"Is that your experience talking, or your hormones, Malone?"

He didn't intend to dignify that question with an answer. "I've gotten to know her pretty well these last couple of weeks, Elaine. Her father's reputation was impeccable and Claire is a dedicated professional. This research study is important to her."

"And this case is important to me," Elaine replied. "Now tell me what's happening on your end."

Mitch stepped farther under the eaves as lightning flashed in the sky. "I've talked with all the employees at The Jungle and put out feelers about scoring some bootleg Viagra, but no hits yet. I don't think any of the staff is involved. Next on my list is the liquor distributor and the other vendors. I need to talk to the cleaning crew, too, and then dig up the names of some former disgruntled employees. Maybe one of them will be willing to talk."

"Sounds like you're keeping busy."

"Day and night," he said, rubbing the back of his neck. "I'm either on bouncer duty at the club, working the case, or out with Claire on interviews."

"Learn anything interesting on those interviews?"

"Much more than I ever wanted to know," Mitch said honestly. "We've got an amazing number of sexual fetishists living in this city. Most of them are harmless, though."

"Is Dick Vandalay on the interview list?"

"Yes, but Claire's talking to him only after she's through interviewing all the other research subjects." The drizzle turned into a downpour and he saw people on the sidewalks running for cover. "Albert Ramirez is the last one, so we should finish up today if he doesn't cancel again. Then Claire will schedule a time to meet with Vandalay."

"Can't you hurry her up?"

This didn't sound like his partner. She'd always been painfully methodical in their investigations. No doubt she was going stir-crazy during the slow recovery process. "Not without arousing suspicion."

"Didn't you say she's already collected some information on Vandalay?"

"Yeah, his personal history and background information."

"Can you get access to it?"

"She's got it on her computer," Mitch replied. "Along with the rest of her research project."

"She sounds organized," Elaine mused. "Maybe she keeps files on everything—including her business transactions with Vandalay."

"We don't have any proof Claire is involved," Mitch repeated, then realized he sounded defensive. "But as soon as I find a way into her apartment, I'll take a look at all her files."

Static hummed in his ear for a beat. "You've known

this woman for almost a month and you still haven't been to her place? How is that possible?"

"You haven't met her doorman," Mitch replied, glancing at his watch. Claire was five minutes late. Had something delayed her? Was she trying to reach him right now?"

"Look, I'd better go."

"Call me as soon as you learn anything new," Elaine said. "Anything at all. No matter how small."

"I will. Take care of yourself."

She emitted a short laugh. "This physical therapy is so grueling, I'll be able to whip your butt by the time I'm through. And I will, if you don't find a way into the Dellafield woman's apartment soon. Got it, Malone?"

"Loud and clear," he said, then disconnected the phone and slipped it into his belt. Thunder rumbled overhead and he turned to see Claire rushing up the stoop. He caught her by the arms as she slipped on the wet pavement.

"Careful." He liked the feel of her under his hands.

"I'm usually not such a klutz," she said, pushing her wet hair out of her face. Rain glistened on her cheeks, making her skin glow. "You seem to bring it out in me."

"It's another one of my talents." He forced himself to let go of her, then turned to open the door of the brownstone. "After you."

"This is it, Mitch," Claire said, as they climbed the stairs to the fourth floor. "Our last interview."

"Except for Dick Vandalay," he reminded her.

"Right. Only you won't have to be present for that one." She smiled up at him. "I think I'll be safe enough in The Jungle."

He wasn't so sure. Vandalay might pose more danger to her and her career than either one of them realized. He knew Claire was counting on this research study to secure her teaching position at Penleigh College.

That was the difference between them. His career didn't hinge on solving this case. But it might absolve him of the guilt that ate at him over Elaine's accident. Although, lying to Claire didn't exactly make him feel like a hero. Even though she considered him one ever since he'd rescued her from that mugger.

He squared his shoulders as Claire knocked on Ramirez's door. Elaine was right. He needed to find a way into Claire's apartment and get that information on Vandalay. Then he needed to get the hell out of her life.

Before she found out the truth and kicked him out.

CLAIRE SAT AT THE RICKETY table in Albert Ramirez's kitchen. He worked for a laundry service, although the man personally preferred vinyl for his tablecloth instead of linen. The entire room was decorated in early authentic diner, with plenty of pilfered restaurant glasses, ashtrays and salt and pepper sets to prove it. Mitch sat across from her, his arms folded on his broad chest and his long legs stretched out in front of him. He didn't look like he was having much fun.

Albert hadn't been too thrilled when he discovered Mitch standing behind her, either. But he'd rallied nicely and didn't seem at all reluctant to answer the interview questions. In fact, he often provided intimate details that she didn't need, or really want to know.

"We can move on now," Claire interjected, as Albert was describing the favorite positions of a hotel maid he'd met in the Plaza a month ago while making a laundry pickup.

Albert glanced over at Mitch. "Remember that name if you're ever at the Plaza. Gabriella." He heaved a wistful sigh. "Boy, does she give good room service." Then he looked at Claire. "Of course, she's nothing compared to you. You've got a lot of class. That's one of the first things I noticed about you."

After her legs. "Okay, moving on." Claire found it curious that Albert obviously didn't seem to mind the notion of sharing the limber Gabriella with another man. She wondered if Mitch was interested, now that he'd heard about the maid's skills. She decided she didn't want to know.

Claire had finally admitted defeat in her attempts to seduce him. Ever since that kiss at Mrs. Cudahy's two weeks ago, Mitch had kept a polite distance, despite her best efforts to draw him closer.

"Are you sure I can't get you anything?" Albert

asked Claire. "How about some iced tea? Or a glass of wine. I might have a beer in the fridge."

"I'm fine," she said for the third time.

Albert's gaze moved over her body. "You certainly are. Very fine indeed."

Mitch picked up the ashtray in the center of the table. "This looks familiar."

When Claire saw The Jungle logo on in the bottom of it, she glanced up to see Albert's ruddy cheeks grow beet red. "I like to advertise for the nightclub. When my friends come here, they all ask about it."

Mitch nodded slowly. "So you steal restaurant supplies for promotional purposes?"

"I wouldn't use the word steal," Albert said indignantly. "Hotels and restaurants expect their patrons to take things like ashtrays and glasses and towels. Why else do they stamp the name on them?"

"So they can identify stolen property?" Mitch ventured.

Albert shoved back his chair. "I think you'd better leave."

"Mr. Ramirez," Claire began, shooting a warning look at Mitch. "Please sit down. If you'll just answer a few more questions, we'll be through here."

"We're through now," he said huffily. "I don't mind if you stay, Claire. In fact, I'd like it. But I won't be accused of being a thief in my own home."

Mitch narrowed his eyes. "I'll be happy to accuse you somewhere else, Ramirez. How about down at the police station?"

"That's it," Albert shouted, pointing toward the door. "Out!"

She turned to Mitch. "Maybe you should wait out in the hall for me."

"Forget it," he answered in a clipped tone.

"Listen to the lady," Albert said, sidling next to Claire. "She wants to stay with me."

Mitch rose to his feet. "I'm not going anywhere without her."

"We'll just see about that." Albert walked over to the front door and swung it open. "I'm through answering any more questions without my lawyer present."

Claire looked down at her notepad in dismay. "But we're not even halfway done with the interview yet."

"You never told me you'd be bringing along a guard dog," Albert complained. "I thought it would be just you and me."

"I guess you thought wrong." Mitch held out one arm. "Let's go, Claire."

She could see that both Mitch and Ramirez were spoiling for a fight. *Over her?* So instead of pushing the issue, she hastily gathered up her materials and stuffed them in her tote bag. Then she and Mitch walked out the door, her bare legs feeling the breeze as it slammed behind them.

"What a jerk," Mitch exclaimed.

"We'll let him cool down for a few days," Claire said, swinging the tote bag over her shoulder, "then I'll try to reschedule the interview."

He stared at her in disbelief. "You actually want to come back here?"

"It doesn't matter if I want to or not," Claire explained, heading down the narrow staircase to the first floor. "Albert Ramirez is a subject in my study. It will be incomplete without him."

"Can't you just drop him and find a new one?"

"It doesn't work that way." They walked out into the bright afternoon sunshine. A bus pulled away from the curb, leaving a heavy cloud of diesel fumes in its wake. "I've already invested a lot of time cataloging his background and personal data. Besides, when you do a study like this, you have to take what you get."

"The guy is a creep," Mitch said between clenched teeth. "Did you see the way he was looking at you?"

"It's not really his fault," she told him, realizing it was time to explain. She trusted him enough now to know he wouldn't laugh at her. "The skirt's obviously still having an effect on him."

Mitch stared at her. "That's the second time you've mentioned a skirt. I still don't know what you're talking about."

Claire walked to the curb to wait for a taxi. "Do you know what an aphrodisiac is?"

Mitch stiffened at the word, dread filling his chest. "Sure. It's a substance that arouses sexual desire."

"Well, the black skirt I wore to The Jungle that first night has a special thread running through it made from the fiber of a rare root in the Caribbean. It has incredibly strong aphrodisiac powers. It's the reason you kissed me that night."

"Like hell," he said, even as Elaine's words echoed in his head. *Claire Dellafield has had plenty of opportunity to make connections with the sort of people who traffic in illegal aphrodisiacs.*

"It's true." Claire hailed a taxi, but it sped by her. "That's also why the cabbie followed me into the rest room and why those men started the brawl." She smiled up at him. "Believe me, that's the first time in my life men have ever fought over me."

He couldn't believe it. He didn't want to believe it. Not when he'd already convinced himself that Claire had nothing to do with this case. His mind whirled when he realized she'd practically just confessed to him.

"But I still don't understand your behavior with Ramirez just now," she said, unaware of the turmoil she'd just unleashed inside of him. "You sounded more like a cop than a bouncer."

He smiled, his lips stiff. "You're right. I guess I just don't like seeing Jungle property scattered across the five boroughs. Sorry if I screwed up your research project."

"It's all right," she said, taking another stab at hailing a taxi.

"No, it's not." He took a step closer, knowing he had to be certain she was involved before he did anything drastic. That meant finding a way into her apartment for some solid evidence. "I'd like to make it up to you. Let me take you out to dinner tonight."

"You don't have to do that," Claire protested half-heartedly.

"I want to," he replied. And he meant it. He'd been spending time with Claire to try and prove her guilty of a crime. Now he was determined to prove her innocent.

A cab pulled up beside the curb and Mitch opened the door for her. "Go home and put on your best dress. We're going someplace special. I'll pick you up at eight."

Before Claire could even open her mouth, Mitch closed the door and the taxi took off down the street. He watched it until it was out of sight, apprehension churning in his gut. If Claire was involved in this case, he needed to find out as soon as possible.

Then figure out what the hell to do about it.

12

CLAIRE STARED INSIDE HER closet, wondering what to wear for an apology date. Sam's special black skirt tempted her, but now that Mitch knew about its powers, she couldn't be so obvious. Why had she ever opened her big mouth?

"It doesn't matter," she muttered aloud, pulling a simple black cocktail dress out of the closet. She added the rose silk scarf, so Franco wouldn't nag her when they left the building. He'd insisted all the girls wear scarves ever since he'd done their colors.

When she was fully dressed, down to her new pair of designer shoes, she brushed out her long hair, then stood in front of the mirror while her fingers worked it into a French braid. She was half done when the doorbell rang. Surprised, her gaze swung to the clock on the bathroom wall. It was only seven-thirty. And she didn't have a molecule of makeup on yet.

The doorbell rang a second time and Claire told herself it was probably just Mrs. Higgenbotham wanting to tell them about some change in Cleo's schedule. With Sam and A.J. already out for the evening, Claire walked into the living room with her hands still tangled in her hair to hold the intricate braid in place. As she stared in dismay at the locked door, the bell rang again and Claire realized she had no choice but to let the braid unravel so she could open the door.

Unfortunately, it wasn't Mrs. Higgenbotham on the other side. It was Mitch. Half an hour early. She'd always hated punctual people.

Only it was impossible to hate him.

He stood there looking sinfully handsome in a gray suit and a blue tie that matched his eyes, holding a bouquet of pink roses. His gaze wandered down her body in a way that made her feel better about leaving the black skirt in Samantha's closet. "Wow."

A tingle of pleasure suffused her. "Come on in. I'm not quite ready yet."

"These are for you," he said, holding out the flowers. "My way of saying I'm sorry about this afternoon."

Apology flowers. The tingle faded at the reminder that this wasn't a real date. She'd probably just imagined that spark of desire in his deep blue eyes. A pitiful case of wishful thinking. "They're beautiful. Let me put them in some water."

"Great place," he said, looking around as he walked inside. "I've never been inside a Central Park West apartment before. Would you mind giving me the full tour?"

She'd rather give him a blindfold until she had a chance to fix her hair and apply some makeup. But since he'd already seen her in all her disshelved glory, what did it really matter? "Follow me."

Claire led him into the kitchen first, where she placed the two dozen roses in a vase Petra had made for her. Mitch admired the dark cherry cabinets and ran one hand over the sleek black granite countertop. "Nice."

Then she led him down the hallway. "A.J.'s room is over there. And Sam sleeps in here. It's got the best view of Central Park."

"Sam?" he said tightly, his eyes narrowed. "Does he sleep alone?"

Claire smiled and the tingle flickered once more. "Yes, *she* does. The three of us are subletting this apartment together for the summer."

Claire led him into the media room, grateful she had tidied it up this afternoon. "This is where I sleep. This room was already set up for a computer, so it's a handy place for me to work."

His gaze took in the small room. "But the sofa doesn't look too cozy."

"It folds out into a queen-size bed. Plenty of room for more than one person." Why had she said *that*? Before he could respond, she spun on her heel and headed out the door. "Go ahead and make yourself comfortable, Mitch. I'll be ready in a few minutes."

She knew it would take at least that long to yank her foot out of her mouth.

MITCH COULDN'T BELIEVE IT was this easy. He was standing in Claire's bedroom within three feet of her computer. His long experience with women had told him she wouldn't be ready for a date this early. But he hadn't expected to gain access to her data so quickly.

He waited until he heard the bathroom door close down the hallway, then he pulled up a chair and sat down at the computer desk. It only took him a moment to find the power button, then he tapped his fingers impatiently against the mouse pad as it fired up.

"Come on, come on," he muttered.

The screen blinked on as the files began to load. Now he just had to find the right one.

"Hey, Mitch?" Claire called out from the bathroom.

He popped out of the chair and moved toward the door. "Yeah?"

"I think someone is at the front door. Would you mind getting it for me?

Damn. He'd been so focused on finding Vandalay's file, he hadn't even heard the bell. "Sure."

With a sigh of reluctance, he switched off the computer, then moved into the living room to open the door. An older woman stood on the other side holding a magnum bottle of champagne.

"You must be Mitch Malone." She beamed up at him. "I'm Petra Gerard. I live next door. Claire's told me so much about you." She peered around the doorway. "Am I interrupting anything?"

"Not at all," he said, holding the door open wider.

"That's too bad." She walked inside, then handed

him the champagne bottle. "Go ahead and open this for me, please. We need to celebrate."

Mitch looked down at the label, impressed with the vintage. "I'll see if I can find a corkscrew in the kitchen."

"We'll need three wineglasses, too," she called after him.

Naturally, the corkscrew was in the last drawer Mitch looked in. He found the wineglasses right away though, and carried them all back into the living room.

Petra's gaze followed him as he set the glasses on the coffee table. "I wouldn't call them morning glories."

"What?" Mitch tore off the foil paper on top of the bottle, then twisted the corkscrew into the cork.

"Your eyes. I think cornflower would be a closer match. Of course, the right lighting can make all the difference in the world."

He had no idea what she was talking about. Before he could ask, Claire walked into the living room. She'd tamed her long hair into a fancy braid, and while he found it attractive, he liked the way she'd worn it before even better. Loose and wild. As if she'd just tumbled out of that roomy sofa bed.

"Petra," Claire said, stumbling to a halt when saw her neighbor. "What are you doing here?"

Petra clasped her hands together. "My, you do look pretty tonight, Claire." Then she turned to Mitch. "Doesn't she look pretty?"

"Very pretty," he said, carefully sliding the cork out of the bottle. It popped and champagne foamed out of the top.

Claire scooped up the glasses and held them under the lip of the bottle before any of the champagne spilled onto the carpet.

"We were just on our way out to dinner," Claire explained, handing one of the glasses to Petra.

"Well, before you go, you must drink a toast with me." The woman's green eyes sparkled with excitement. "I just signed for a showing at the Ledbetter Gallery!"

"That's wonderful," Claire reached out to give Petra a hug. "I'm so proud of you!"

The two women clung to each other and Mitch realized that this must be the godmother Claire had mentioned—a former professor at Penleigh. He'd learned that the faculty there was like her family. The college campus, the only home she'd ever really known.

Petra kissed her cheek. "The showing is in three weeks. You will be my guest of honor."

Claire turned to Mitch. "Petra is the most wonderful sculptress."

"I'm impressed." He filled the remaining two glasses with champagne, then handed one of them to Claire. "Congratulations."

"Thank you," Petra replied, lifting her glass in the air. "Claire, your father always gave the best toasts.

Now I'd like nothing better than for his daughter to toast this very special occasion in my life."

"To success," Claire toasted, holding her glass up in the air. "In art. In life. In love."

"Success," Petra cried out with relish as they took turns clinking their glasses together.

Petra drained her glass, then threw it into the fireplace, where it exploded into tiny pieces. Then she motioned to Mitch to do the same.

"Hold it." Claire grabbed his elbow. "These wineglasses belong to A.J."

"I'll buy her a new set," Petra promised. "Now we must follow tradition and break the glasses."

Mitch looked at Claire, who shrugged, then drained her glass before tossing it into the cold hearth. He followed her example. The shards of glass glittered against the gray brick.

Mitch looked up from the fireplace to see Petra staring at him. After the odd remark about cornflowers, he wondered if she was completely stable. Then again, most of the artists he knew were a little flaky.

"Mitch is the spitting image of Delmore," she said at last.

"Delmore?" Mitch echoed, looking from one woman to the other.

Petra turned to Claire. "You remember Delmore? That model who took off for San Francisco in the middle of our sittings?"

Claire crinkled her brow. "No."

"Well, he left me high and dry," Petra exclaimed.

"If I could finish that sculpture, I know it would be the hit of the show."

Understanding dawned on Claire's face. "I really don't think that's such a good idea."

"Why don't we let Mitch decide. He's a big boy." Petra whirled on him. "Please say you'll do it."

"Do what exactly?" he asked, looking back and forth between the two of them.

"Pose for me so I can finish the sculpture." Then seeing his expression, she modified her request. "Or just let me take a few pictures of you so I have something to work with. I'm a very visual person. I need to see the object I'm trying to create."

"I don't think Mitch is the right man for you," Claire began, obviously trying to give him an out.

He appreciated it, but what would it hurt to let the old lady snap a few pictures? It would make her happy. And it was obvious that she and Claire were very close. It might even help assuage the uneasiness he felt about using this date to gain access to Claire's computer files. "Okay, I'll do it."

Petra clapped her hands together. "Wonderful! I'll go get my camera."

Mitch watched her sprint toward the door, amazed a woman her age could move so fast. When she was gone, he turned to Claire. "Petra is something else."

"You have no idea," Claire replied with a wry smile. She walked into the kitchen, then returned with more wineglasses and poured them each another glass of champagne. "I think you're going to need this."

"That sounds ominous."

She looked up at him, amusement dancing in her brown eyes. "There's something you should know about Petra's sculptures."

He lifted his wineglass to his mouth. "What?"

But before she could tell him, Petra burst back into the apartment with an instant camera in one hand and a scrap of black leather in the other. "Here you go. You can change in Claire's room."

He stared down at the black thong she'd just handed him, and apprehension bubbled in his stomach along with the champagne. "Change?"

"For the pictures," she said simply.

He looked closer at it, realizing it wasn't a thong, but rather a modified version, with a flap of fabric hanging in both the back and front.

"It's a loincloth," Petra explained, seeing Mitch's confusion. "Like in *Tarzan*. Have you never seen it?"

"Not quite like this." He held the thong up to the light. "Delmore modeled for you in this?"

"Oh my, no." Petra laughed. "I usually insist that all my models pose in the nude. But since this is your first date with Claire, I didn't think that would be appropriate."

He glanced at his date, who sat watching him over the rim of her champagne glass. He couldn't quite read the expression in her beautiful eyes.

"As I said before," Petra continued, "the project is

already half done. I always do my favorite parts first. Which leaves only the shoulders and upper thighs left to sculpt."

Favorite parts? He decided he didn't want to know.

"Hurry now," Petra said, waving him down the hallway. "I'm sure you're both getting hungry."

Claire arched a brow in his direction, obviously expecting him to back out.

She was in for a big surprise.

13

CLAIRE COULDN'T BELIEVE Mitch actually went through with it—loincloth and all. Petra positioned him on the living-room sofa in a half-reclined position, then gingerly adjusted the loincloth, effectively concealing everything Claire really wanted to see.

In sheer sexiness, Mitch had Tarzan beat hands down. *Jane, eat your heart out.*

"Okay, hold it right there...." Petra held up the camera, preparing to snap the first picture. But nothing happened. She pulled the camera away from her face and frowned down at it. "That's strange."

"What's wrong?" Claire asked.

"It doesn't seem to be working." Petra turned it upside down. "I've got film. I've got batteries. I just don't seem to have any power."

"Let me take a look," Mitch said, rising off the sofa.

Claire's mouth went dry as she saw all those muscles shift and bunch as he walked over to Petra. The leather loincloth molded like a second skin to the enticing parts of his body it was supposed to conceal, leaving absolutely nothing to the imagination.

She feasted on him while his back was to her as he fidgeted with the camera. From the wide breadth of his shoulders, to his tapered waist and the firm buttocks beneath. His thighs were thick and solid, all muscle. Every inch of the man was downright delectable, right down to his toes. She had an irrational urge to nip the dark stretch of skin on the back of his neck.

But maybe she was just hungry.

"I don't know what's wrong with it," he said, handing the camera back to Petra.

"It's the only camera I have, too," she said with a defeated sigh. Then a spark lit her eyes. "Unless…"

Claire recognized that look. Petra was definitely plotting something. "Unless what?"

"Unless Mitch would agree to just pose here in the apartment for me." She held up both hands before either one of them could say anything. "I know you two have dinner plans, but I'd be happy to order takeout from Jean Georges. I promise you two will hardly even know that I'm here."

Disappointment washed over Claire. She'd been looking forward to an intimate dinner with Mitch. Then she reminded herself this wasn't a real date. "It's up to Mitch."

"What do you say?" Petra asked, turning to him. "Jean Georges is fabulous. I know the head chef personally. And we can't let the rest of this champagne go to waste."

Mitch hesitated, then shrugged. "I guess I don't mind if it's all right with Claire."

"Of course," Claire said more cheerfully than she felt. "I'll just set the table."

"And I'll go to my apartment and get the sculpture," Petra said, moving toward the door. "I'll call the restaurant while I'm there and order dinner for two. I'm sure I can convince the chef to prepare something extra special."

"Dinner for two?" Claire said. "Aren't you eating with us?"

"No, thank you, dear. I'm fasting." Petra left the door cracked open as she moved into the hallway.

Claire walked into the kitchen, telling herself it was better this way. She didn't want Mitch spending his hard-earned money on her. No doubt the evening would end early and she could get some work done. That's why she'd come to New York City, she reminded herself. To work, not play.

So why did she feel like throwing every glass in the apartment into the fireplace?

The kitchen door swung open and she turned to see Mitch standing there in his loincloth.

"Need some help?" he asked.

A fire extinguisher would be nice. Then it struck her how ridiculous this evening was turning out. She didn't know whether to laugh or drool. "You can set out the silverware. It's in the drawer by the stove."

Claire watched him out of the corner of her eye, the flap of the loincloth offering tantalizing glimpses of what lay underneath. A sip of champagne helped cool her blood—until he dropped a fork and bent down to pick it up.

Claire started to choke as the champagne bubbles went down the wrong way. It didn't help matters when Mitch rushed over and started pounding on her back.

"Are you okay?" he asked, standing so close to her that the edge of the leather loincloth rubbed against her fingertips.

She thought about swooning into his arms in the hope that he'd give her mouth-to-mouth resuscitation, but Petra chose that moment to stick her head in the kitchen door. "It's all set. The food will be here in an hour. Just enough time for me to put the finishing touches on my sculpture. I can't wait to sink my hands into you, Mitch."

Join the club. "You two go ahead and get started," Claire said. "I want to tidy up the kitchen a little bit."

Mitch gave her a lingering look, then padded out of the kitchen in his bare feet. Claire turned on the tap, then squirted dish soap into the sink, watching the bubbles rise to the surface of the water. She really knew how to show a guy a good time.

An hour later, Petra walked through the kitchen door. Her hands were gray with clay and she looked like she wanted to strangle someone.

"Isn't Mitch cooperating?" Claire asked, wiping off the black and white ceramic wall tiles.

"He's performed perfectly so far. You, on the other hand, are driving me crazy."

Claire gaped at her. "Me?"

Petra swung her arm in the direction of the living room. "You've got an incredibly sexy, nearly naked man stretched out on your sofa and where are you? Holed up in the kitchen cleaning the tile grout with a toothbrush."

Claire turned to the shiny backsplash. "It does look whiter now, doesn't it?"

Petra lowered her voice a notch. "Did you or did you not ask for my advice about seducing Mitch?"

"I did," Claire admitted. "But I thought you were joking when you said one or both of us should be naked."

"I never joke about nudity. But now that the man *is* almost naked, how is my plan ever going to work if you're hiding out in here?"

Claire planted her hands on her hips. "There's no way you could have planned all of this. I didn't even tell you Mitch was taking me out tonight."

"I saw him walk out of the elevator when I opened the door to get my newspaper. Since I knew Sam and A.J. both had other plans tonight, I was hoping this meant you two were going to take advantage of the empty apartment. But I decided to stop by just to make sure."

Claire shook her head in disbelief. "So that whole bit with the champagne and the Ledbetter Gallery and Delmore taking off for San Francisco was just a ruse?"

"No, that was true. Well, everything but the part about Delmore. Mitch's body is definitely superior, though, so I'm happy it all worked out this way."

Claire silently counted to ten. She loved Petra, but she didn't need this kind of help. If Mitch found out this was all a setup.... She groaned low in her throat, then gently pushed Petra toward the door. "Go home. I'll handle the rest of the evening on my own."

"Good idea. I've done my part. Oh that reminds me, I put some condoms in the drawer of your nightstand. Just in case." The doorbell rang and Petra's eyes lit up. "There's the food. I ordered entrées with lots of carbohydrates so Mitch will have plenty of energy for the night ahead."

"You and I are going to have a long talk tomorrow," Claire told her.

"Wonderful. I can't wait to hear all the juicy details." Petra pushed open the kitchen door and Claire followed her out in time to see a delivery boy handing Mitch two large plastic cartons. Then he pulled the bill out of the front pocket of his uniform.

"I'll take that," Petra called, waving her hand in the air as she walked toward the door.

"No, let me. I promised to treat Claire to dinner tonight." Mitch reached for his wallet, then realized he wasn't wearing any pants.

"Don't be ridiculous," Petra replied, snatching the

bill from the delivery boy's hand. "It's the least I could do after changing your plans at the last moment."

Mitch moved toward the bedroom where he'd left his clothes. "At least let me pay the tip."

But Petra had already steered the delivery boy out the door. They could hear her voice echoing down the hallway. "Have you ever done any modeling, young man? I think you'd be a natural...."

Mitch turned to Claire. "Do you mind if I dress for dinner?"

She treated herself to one last look. "Go right ahead. I'll get the food ready while you're changing."

Tantalizing aromas drifted upward as she opened the first carton. Using a fork already on the table, she slid the tender roasted squab onto a plate, then scraped the succulent sauce out on top of it.

"They're gone."

She looked up to see Mitch standing just inside the living room, still wearing the loincloth. "What?"

"My clothes," he said, moving closer to the table. "I can't find them anywhere."

Claire rounded the table and headed down the hallway to her room. But Mitch was right. His clothes were nowhere in sight. "Where did you put them?"

He stood in the doorway of her bedroom, leaning one elbow against the frame. "Right there on the sofa."

"Well, they have to be around here somewhere."

But as she bent over to look behind the sofa, an awful thought struck her. *Petra.* Claire straightened and saw the same suspicion gleaming in Mitch's eyes.

"Why would she take my clothes?" he asked.

Claire moistened her lips, trying to come up with a reasonable explanation. Instead, she settled for the truth. "I'm afraid this is Petra's version of matchmaking."

He grinned. "Subtle."

"Mitch, I'm so sorry about all of this." She picked up the telephone. "I'll call her right now and tell her to bring your clothes back here immediately."

But thirty rings later, Claire gave up. "Either she's not answering the phone or she's not home."

"She's probably on a date with that delivery boy." He took a step closer to her. "Look, there's no use letting all that great food get cold. Why don't we go ahead and eat now, then track down Petra later."

"Good idea." Claire's gaze flicked downward. "Can I get you a robe or something?"

He shook his head. "I doubt it will fit. I'm a lot bigger than you."

Especially where it counted. "Then I guess you get to play Tarzan for a little while longer."

"You can just call me lord of The Jungle."

"Cute," she said, walking out of her bedroom. "Very cute."

THREE HOURS LATER, MITCH was still wearing the loincloth, but playing a different game.

"My teeth feel soft," he said, reclining on the sofa with his head propped in his hands.

"Okay, let me think a minute." Claire sat cross-legged on the carpet, her back leaning against the sofa. She was so close he could stretch out his hand and touch the silky curls of her hair. Or lean his head down a few inches and graze the creamy skin on her neck with his lips. No doubt that would be against the rules.

They'd been playing the game for the last couple of hours. Bouncing movie lines off each other, with each right answer worth one point. Claire kept score on a spare paper napkin from Jean Georges. So far Mitch was winning by three points.

"Give up?" he asked.

She snapped her fingers, glancing back at him with a triumphant grin. *"Barefoot in the Park."*

"Correct," he said grudgingly, watching her add another point to her score. He'd always been competitive, but Mitch had met his match. "Okay, your turn."

"I can be smart when it's important."

Mitch shook his head. "I haven't a clue."

"Gentlemen Prefer Blondes," Claire said, marking down another point.

Not this gentleman. At the moment, he definitely favored brunettes. He'd love to see how her hair looked spread across a pillow. Or brushing over his chest. His hips. Which led his thoughts in a direction that no gentleman would ever go.

Claire glanced up at him. "Your turn."

He cleared his throat and recited the first movie line that popped into his head. "It's beyond my control."

"That's easy," Claire replied, marking down another point. "*Dangerous Liaisons*."

It was also a sign of where he was headed if he didn't stop thinking about making love to Claire. Any liaison with her would be dangerous, not only to his case, but to his heart. She could never be a woman he could take to bed, then forget. Claire Dellafield was already branded into his brain and all he'd ever done was kiss her.

But he wanted to do so much more.

"I'm enormously attracted to you." she said.

He blinked, his body going into full alert. "What?"

"I'm enormously attracted to you." Then she arched a finely winged brow. "Give up?"

The game. She was talking about the game. He took a deep breath, his heart beating so fast he feared it might explode. For a moment, he thought she'd just issued him an invitation and he'd almost accepted it. Almost pulled Claire into his arms and shown her just how much he wanted her.

His lower body throbbed and he hastily reached for the coverlet on the back of the sofa and draped it over his waist before she could see what could no longer be concealed by the skimpy loincloth.

"Cold?" she asked.

"A little," he lied, as perspiration beaded on his forehead. She looked cool and composed. As well as fully dressed.

He'd love to correct that situation by slowly unzipping that sexy black dress she wore until it slipped off her body and pooled at her feet. Then he'd unhook her bra so he could cup her full breasts in his hands. He'd linger there for a while, letting his mouth and tongue enjoy the delicacies she had to offer before trailing his fingers down her waist and over her hips until they snagged in her panties. He'd kiss his way down her luscious body, sliding them off, until she stood completely naked before him.

"Time's up," Claire said, interrupting the fantasy.

He licked his parched lips, realizing he should have surrendered a long time ago. "I give up."

"The movie is *Surrender*." She flashed a smile. "That's another point for me."

That smile hit him right in the solar plexus. Mitch had never desired a woman more and he wasn't even touching her. Claire Dellafield was stimulating in so many different ways. To his mind. His competitive streak. His body. Definitely his body.

She turned to look at him, her mouth temptingly close to his own. "Don't you find it amazing that we've both seen so many of the same movies?"

All he had to do was tilt his head a fraction of an

inch and he could kiss her. "I think it means we've both got great taste."

Her eyes met his and neither one of them said anything for a long moment. He could feel her warm breath against his cheek and it was coming even faster than before. Up this close, he saw the gold flecks in her brown eyes and her incredibly long lashes. If he didn't do something soon, he was going to kiss her and forget the real reason he'd come here tonight—to take a look at her computer files.

"It's hot, isn't it?"

"Then take off the blanket," Claire replied, feeling a little hot herself. Maybe it was the way he was looking at her. Or the odd drape of the blanket over his hips that did little to conceal his arousal.

So why didn't he do anything about it? Like kiss her? Or rip off her clothes? *Why didn't she?*

"That was a movie line," he told her, leaning his head back to give her an even better view of the broad expanse of his chest. Her gaze roamed over his flat nipples and the washboard muscles below his ribs. The sight of his navel at the top of the blanket gave the illusion that he was completely naked underneath it.

She cleared her throat, realizing too late that she'd been staring. Lifting her gaze up to his face, she asked, "Can you repeat it, please?"

His blue eyes darkened. "It's hot, isn't it?"

Unbearable. "*Body Heat?*"

"A great movie," he said huskily.

She nodded. "Very hot."

"Steamy," he agreed, as the temperature in the apartment seemed to spike up about fifty degrees.

A drop of perspiration trickled beneath her breasts and Claire itched to take off her dress. What if she stood up right now and asked Mitch to unzip her? To make love to her? She rose to her feet, her knees shaky.

His gaze followed her as she shook her hair off her shoulders. Then she took a deep breath, her heart hammering in her chest. "I need you."

He stared up at her for a long moment. *"Funny Lady."*

The game. She'd meant to give him her body and inadvertantly given him another movie line. Although she didn't remember that particular line from the movie. Maybe it didn't exist. Maybe he'd guessed her intent to seduce him and tried the only way he knew how to dissuade her. To let her down easy.

She took a step away from him and tried to breathe normally. "You win, Mitch."

He didn't say anything for a long moment, then sat up farther on the sofa. "I wonder if Petra is back yet."

"I'll go over to her apartment and check," she replied, moving for the door. She needed to get away from him and clear her head. "Franco probably would have let us in there with his passkey if you hadn't made that crack about his shoes."

"They caught me off guard." Mitch explained,

shifting on the sofa but keeping the coverlet strategically placed over his hips. "I'm not used to a doorman wearing ruby slippers."

Claire placed her hand on the doorknob. "And I can't believe a man who watches so many movies has never even seen *The Wizard of Oz*."

"Well, nobody's perfect."

"*Some Like It Hot*." she exclaimed, turning in the doorway. "Now we're tied. Game over." Then she walked out into the hallway.

Mitch watched her disappear, wishing it was true. But the real game was just beginning.

14

"NOW, DON'T BE MAD," Petra said, handing Claire the stack of Mitch's neatly folded clothes. "Just tell me if it worked. Did you and Mitch..."

"No," Claire replied. "We ate dinner, which was fabulous by the way, thank you. Then we played a game."

Petra's brows rose. "What kind of game?"

"Guess that movie line."

Petra frowned. "I hope you at least played the strip version."

"There is no strip version." Claire shifted the bundle of clothes in her arms. "Besides, Mitch would have been completely naked just by missing one question."

Her eyes gleamed. "Exactly."

Claire turned around and marched back to her apartment without another word. It was more than a little embarrassing to admit that nothing *had* happened. Maybe she should have made the first move—but what if he wasn't interested? They worked well enough together that she didn't want to do anything to jeopardize that.

It was difficult enough to focus on her study with a

fully clothed Mitch around. But now she had his image wearing only a loincloth burned into her brain.

Only when she entered her apartment there was no Mitch to be seen, nearly naked or otherwise. He wasn't in the kitchen, either, or the bathroom. Claire walked down the hallway, where she saw light emanating from underneath her bedroom door. She leaned her ear against it and thought she heard the whir of her computer. Turning the knob, she opened it and saw Mitch standing in front of the lit computer screen.

"What are you doing?"

Mitch froze at the sound of her voice. He'd taken longer than necessary to download one of the files onto a diskette, simply because he hadn't wanted to believe what was right in front of his eyes. Claire had an entire file about aphrodisiacs on her computer. Along with their countries of origin and several names that he didn't recognize.

He clicked off the computer screen button, then turned to face her. "Playing solitaire," he improvised. "But I'm tired of playing alone."

Her brown eyes widened as he stepped toward her, then a soft gasp left her mouth as he pulled her into his arms. He told himself he did it to distract her. To keep her from discovering that he'd been snooping in her computer files. But his body belied any attempt at rationalization. It throbbed with need for her as he bent his head to capture her sweet mouth with his own. Something he'd been wanting to do all night long.

The low moan he heard came from deep within his own chest as she softened against him. She dropped his clothes on the floor, then her hands slid up his bare back. They kneaded his muscles in firm round strokes as he deepened the kiss. Then she grabbed onto his shoulders as her mouth opened for him and his tongue stroked the silky depths inside.

"Mitch," she whispered, as his lips trailed frantically over her jaw and down the length of her neck.

He kissed her again before she could tell him to stop. Before he could tell himself that this was a stupid idea, that someone must have put an aphrodisiac in his food tonight. It would explain why his heart was beating at a lethal rate and his only thoughts were of touching every inch of her. Every naked inch.

His fingers tangled in Claire's silky long hair, crushing her curls, before finding the zipper on the back of her dress. He inched it down as her tongue performed an erotic dance inside his mouth. When the dress finally gaped open, he pushed the sleeves off her shoulders and the dress fell to her hips. He lifted his head and stared into her brown eyes, now wide with desire.

Then he bent his head to kiss the spot where the creamy skin of her breast met the black lace of her bra. Claire threaded her fingers through his hair, encouraging him to take his time there.

He did.

Then she took his hand and led him to the sofa, both of them sinking into the goose-down pillows she had piled there. Mitch lay back, pulling her on top of him, relishing the weight of her body against his throbbing flesh as he kissed her.

His hands slipped under the hem of her dress, sliding it up as he smoothed his fingers over her inner thighs. When his fingers encountered the silk of her panties, she lifted her head and closed her eyes with a breathless sigh.

He shifted slightly so that loincloth met panties, firm leather sliding against soft silk.

She moaned aloud at the sensation, so he did it again, his own control stretched to the limit. He loved watching her. Loved the way her lips parted as she flexed her hips against him, riding a wave of pleasure.

"Oh, yes," she gasped, as his fingers slid under the silk. He found more tempting curls and moist, damp heat.

"Mitch," Claire moaned as his fingers sought paradise. Then her breath caught in her throat as she arched against him again and he watched the rapture play over her features before she collapsed against him.

He lay very still, his muscles stiff from resisting the urge to thrust against her. He'd only meant to kiss her. To distract her. When had it all spiraled out of control?

His body throbbed, but he knew he couldn't let this

go any further. Not with that damn diskette still whirring in the A drive of her computer.

Then Claire kissed him, her fingers finding their way into his loincloth and Mitch was lost.

One slender hand curled around him and he groaned at the exquisite sensation. She pushed the leather thong down past his thighs, opening up for him at the same time.

He bent his head to her breasts, tasting each delicate coral nipple as she stroked him. When he was almost to the point of no return, she reached into the nightstand drawer and pulled out a condom.

He bit down hard on his lip as she took her sweet time rolling it on. Then she lay back down on the sofa and held her arms out to him.

He sank into her soft body as her hips rose to meet him.

A quiver shot through him when he saw her watching him. Her big brown eyes full of desire.

And trust.

"Claire," he breathed, thrusting inside of her. The sensation pushed him to the edge, but he forced himself back again, not wanting this perfect moment to end.

He loved watching her eyes flutter closed and her head arch back as she sought the ecstasy his body promised her.

He murmured words of passion in her ear as he made love to her. Mitch, who had always considered talking a waste of time with a woman, now couldn't seem to stop. He told her how much he wanted her. How incredible she felt under him. How he wanted to slow down.

"No," she cried, increasing the rhythm between them of her own accord, until he couldn't think at all anymore.

His own release came a scant moment after hers, waves of pleasure roiling through him as she tightly gripped his shoulders. Mitch held her against him until his breathing finally slowed. Then he rolled onto his side, still holding her in his arms.

He liked the way she curled into him. Inhaling the sweet scent of her hair, he rested his hand against the curve of her breast. Then he nuzzled his face into the crook of her neck, wanting her all over again.

"I think you must have put something in my food," he teased, though he knew the real truth in his heart. "I can't ever remember feeling this way before."

"Me, either," Claire breathed, her voice heavy with sleepy satisfaction.

Mitch lay awake for a long time, holding Claire as she nodded off to sleep. Now that his passion was temporarily slaked, he was all too aware of that diskette still in her computer drive. Mitch finally had what he'd sought from the beginning—evidence to tie her to the case. Which only made his next move even more difficult. If he showed Elaine the information on that computer diskette, she'd believe it was enough evidence to prove Claire's guilt.

He couldn't let that happen.

Mitch leaned forward to gently kiss the back of her head, her hair tickling his nose. Despite all his good intentions, he'd let a woman distract him again. Only it was even worse this time.

Because he'd also fallen in love with her.

THE NEXT MORNING CLAIRE awoke to find herself nestled in Mitch's strong arms. They'd unfolded the sofa bed sometime during the night, then made a serious dent in the condom supply.

She snuggled closer to him, relishing his warmth and inhaling his unique masculine scent.

"Good morning," he murmured, his voice still gruff from sleep.

"Good isn't the right word for it," she replied, tilting her head to look up at him. "Wonderful. Fantastic. Incredible."

He leaned forward to kiss the tip of her nose. "That's funny. Those are the exact words I'd use to describe you."

Claire cradled her head against his shoulder. "Let's just stay in bed all day."

"Great idea. We can watch videos. Do you suppose Franco will let us borrow *The Wizard of Oz?*"

"I'm sure he would," she replied, as one hand trickled over his chest and down the length of torso. "The only problem is that one of us will have to get out of bed to ask him."

"Forget that," Mitch said, rolling on top of her. Then he froze, his gaze fixed on the wall above her. "What day is this?"

She craned her neck to see him looking at the calendar. "Thursday. July second. Why?"

He groaned, dropping his head into the crook of his

neck. "Because I promised Mrs. Cudahy I'd be there to help her move. The truck is coming at ten o'clock this morning. What time is it now?"

She glanced at the clock on her nightstand. "Nine-thirty."

He nibbled the side of her neck, then rolled off her with a reluctant groan. "Don't move. I'll be back in six hours."

She smiled, her heart bursting with love for a man who would keep a promise to his elderly neighbor. "I'll be right here."

Mitch sat up and reached for his clothes, still piled on the floor where she'd dropped them the night before. "I have an even better idea. Why don't you come with me?"

"I'd love to," she replied, seriously tempted. "But I really should stay in today and get some work down."

"All right. I'll bring takeout for supper. We can eat it in bed." He pulled the shirt over his head and she enjoyed watching the play of muscles in his back.

"And I'll get *The Wizard of Oz* from Franco. We can have our own movie marathon tonight."

Fully dressed now, he leaned over her, one hand braced on either side of her head. "That's not the kind of marathon I have in mind," he said huskily. Then he leaned down to kiss her, his mouth making all kinds of wonderful promises.

"Hurry back," she called after him as he walked out the door. Then she stretched leisurely on the sofa bed, the cotton sheets still warm from his body. She closed her eyes, recalling every sensuous moment of the night before.

A few minutes later, her cell phone rang, dragging her from a blissful haze of half sleep. She reached out one hand to the nightstand, fumbling blindly until she finally found it.

"Hello?"

"Is this Claire?"

She half sat up, trying to place the vaguely familiar voice. "Yes. Who is this?"

"Albert. Albert Ramirez."

"Oh. Hello." She hadn't heard from him since that disastrous interview a week ago and he hadn't returned any of her telephone calls. "How are you, Mr. Ramirez?"

"Fine. Busy, though." Two beats of silence. "I got your messages and I am willing to give you another chance to finish the interview if you're still interested."

Claire sat up and swung her legs over the side of the bed. "I'm very interested. What time works best for you?"

"How about right now?" he suggested. "We could meet at Hal's Diner on Thirty-second Street. My uncle owns it, so I know we can get a table."

"That sounds perfect," she said, running her fingers through the tangles in her hair. "Just give me about twenty minutes."

"Are you planning to bring that Malone character with you?"

"Mitch is busy this morning," she replied, not wanting to scare him off. "So I'll be on my own."

"Wonderful. I'll see you there." Albert said, then hung up.

Claire threw on a pair of khaki shorts and a blue plaid cotton shirt, then quickly combed out her hair before sweeping it into a ponytail. Grabbing her tote bag, she slipped on her sandals then headed for the door. Only to find Mrs. Higgenbotham and Cleo on the other side.

"Just in time," Mrs. Higgenbotham said, holding out the leash. "Cleo was getting antsy."

Claire looked down in dismay at the little white poodle staring up at her. "Oh, I'm sorry, but now is not a good time. I have an appointment."

"You also have a contract that says you or one of your roommates are supposed to walk my dog."

"Maybe Sam or A.J. can do it," she replied, not even sure if her roommates were home. She hadn't heard either one of them come in last night. Of course, she'd had other things on her mind.

"I'll walk Cleo next time," Claire said, heading down the hallway. "I promise."

Mrs. Higgenbotham was still sputtering as the elevator doors closed.

Thirty minutes later, Claire arrived at the diner and saw Albert Ramirez seated in a back booth.

"Sorry I'm late," she said, slipping into the padded bench seat opposite him.

"No problem." He motioned to the plate in front of her, brimming with eggs, sausages, hash browns and a blueberry muffin. "I took the liberty of ordering breakfast for us. I thought it might save time."

"Thank you." She and Mitch had raided the refrigerator in the middle of the night, so she couldn't work up much of an appetite. She nibbled on the muffin before retrieving the interview form out of her tote bag.

"Do you mind if we go ahead and get started?" she asked, as Albert dug into his hash browns.

"Not at all." Then he smiled up at her, the effect ruined by the piece of scrambled egg caught in his teeth. "You look very sexy today."

She cleared her throat. "Thank you."

His expression made her a little uneasy. Maybe she should have asked Mitch to come along after all. But he'd already promised to help Mrs. Cudahy this morning.

She turned her attention to his interview form. "There are only a few questions left, so it shouldn't take long."

"I've cleared my whole day for you," he informed her. "I was hoping we might find something to do together afterward."

"Mr. Ramirez," she said, keeping her tone gentle but firm, "that's not going to happen. As a researcher, I must keep all interactions with my subjects strictly professional."

"We'll see," he said, winking at her as he scooped up a forkful of eggs. "You might change your mind."

"I won't."

"We'll see," he said again.

Time to move on. "Question number eleven," she began automatically, her mind drifting to thoughts of Mitch. She missed him already. She recited the interview questions, all so familiar to her by now that her mind began to drift as she recorded his answers. How much did last night mean to Mitch? Was it just a fling? Or more?

"Is that it?" Albert asked, scraping the last crumbs of toast off his plate.

She looked down at the interview form to find all of his answers neatly penciled in. "I believe so. Thank you very much for you help."

"It was my pleasure." Then he scowled down at her plate. "You've hardly touched a bite."

"I know," she said with a note of regret. "I'm just really not very hungry this morning."

"At least eat the sausages," Albert encouraged. "My uncle grinds the meat himself."

"I'll get a doggie bag and warm them up when I get home," she promised, signaling for the waitress.

Albert didn't look too happy about it, so Claire paid half the check, then gathered her tote bag and the doggie bag before heading out of the diner.

"Claire, wait up," Albert said, following her. "If you change your mind later, about you know, wanting to get together, just give me a call."

"I'll do that," she said, figuring it was easier than trying to explain why she never would. Because she was a professional.

And because she was in love with Mitch.

That realization hit her as she walked back to The Willoughby. Make that floated back to The Willoughby. Her feet barely touched the ground as she entered the foyer of the building.

Until she saw Franco glaring at her. "Is something wrong?"

"Yes," he said, tilting his chin up. "That little bitch completely ruined my day."

Claire blinked at his language, then realized who he meant. "Cleo?"

"Of course. I was all set to sunbathe and she urinated in my wading pool."

"Oh, no," Claire said, covering her mouth so he wouldn't see her smile.

"It's not funny," Franco protested. "I had to throw the entire pool away and old Higgy refuses to reimburse me. She's furious at you, too," he said with a note of relish. "Because she had to walk Cleo herself today. I heard her muttering something about calling her lawyer to break the lease."

Claire sighed. "I'd better get up there and do damage control. Is she home?"

"Yes," Franco replied. "Unfortunately."

Claire rode the elevator to the sixth floor, trying to think of some way to placate Mrs. Higgenbotham. She'd figured it out by the time she knocked on her neighbor's door.

"Oh, it's you," Mrs. Higgenbotham said when she saw Claire standing in the doorway.

"I just wanted to apologize once again for missing my walk with Cleo." The click of toenails against the porcelain tile foyer announced the dog's arrival.

Claire reached into the doggie bag. "So I brought her a little present." She placed the two lukewarm sausages on the floor.

Cleo pounced on them immediately, licking the floor clean.

"It looks as if your apology is accepted," Mrs. Higgenbotham said with a sniff. "Just don't let it happen again."

Then she closed the door.

Claire heaved a sigh of relief as she turned toward her own apartment, glad she'd avoided possible eviction. This time, anyway.

Of course, eviction might not be all bad if she could move in with Mitch. Just the thought of spending every night in bed with him made her whole body tingle. But that might be getting ahead of herself.

For now, she was just going to take it one night at a time.

15

MITCH HELPED LOAD ALL of Mrs. Cudahy's furniture into the truck her son had hired for the move. It took less than six hours, mainly because Mitch kept up a brisk pace, knowing what awaited him when he was through. He couldn't wait to see Claire again. To hold her again. To prove to himself it all wasn't just a wonderful dream.

Later that afternoon, he'd just stepped out of his shower when the doorbell rang. Pulling on a pair of blue jeans, he toweled his hair as he padded barefoot across the worn shag carpet of his living room to the front door. Elaine stood on the other side, leaning heavily on her crutches.

She looked better than the last time he'd seen her, with more flesh on her frame and roses in her cheeks. The latter probably a result of climbing the front stoop leading up to his apartment building.

"What do you think you're doing up here?" he scolded. "Does Dwayne know you're climbing stairs?"

"Dwayne thinks I'm at my physical therapy session." Then her green eyes narrowed on him. "Why didn't you tell me, Mitch?"

Apprehension tightened his gut. How could she know about Claire already? "Tell you what?"

"Don't play dumb with me," she chided, hobbling into his apartment. "I know you better than anyone. So tell me how long you've known that I might be tied to a desk for the rest of my career."

He raked one hand through his wet hair. "Since the day of the accident."

She gave a brisk nod, as if she already knew the answer. "I suppose you thought you were trying to protect me."

"I thought those doctors might be wrong," Mitch clarified. "You're a hell of an investigator, Elaine. And a fighter. I knew if anyone could pull through an injury like this, it would be you."

"So tell me where you are on this case," she said, abruptly changing the subject.

He knew that meant she was close to breaking down. Elaine didn't like to show her vulnerabilities to anyone, even her own partner. He just hoped she didn't feel the need to act invincible around her husband.

"I don't believe Claire Dellafield is involved—at least not voluntarily."

She arched a skeptical brow. "What makes you so sure?"

He thought of the diskette still stuck in that computer drive. "Because I've gotten to know her over the past several weeks. She's not the type."

"Is that your head talking, Mitch, or some other part of your anatomy?"

His jaw tightened. "Believe me, if you met her, you'd realize she could never be capable of anything remotely criminal."

"I guess we'll find out," Elaine said, hobbling back toward the door.

"What do you mean?"

She glanced over her shoulder. "I got a call about an hour ago from a desk sergeant at the precinct. He's been retrieving records for me about the case."

"And?"

"And he told me they just brought Claire Dellafield in."

A cold wave of fear washed over him. "What for?"

"Possession of an illegal substance."

Mitch stared at her, denial screaming in his brain. "That's ridiculous. She's not guilty of anything." *Except making him fall in love with her.*

"Then she'd better tell us who is," Elaine said, heading out the door. "Or she could be in big trouble."

Mitch followed her, stopping just long enough to grab a shirt and a pair of shoes. He kept picturing the way Claire had looked in bed this morning. So warm and loving.

So innocent.

Now, no matter what it took, he just had to find a way prove it.

CLAIRE PACED BACK AND forth in the small holding room, absently rubbing her wrists. The handcuffs hadn't left a mark, though she'd never forget the humiliating experience of being led out of The Willoughby with her wrists shackled behind her back. Franco had practically fallen out of his lawn chair.

She still couldn't believe she'd been arrested. For drugging Cleo! It just didn't make sense. One minute, Mrs. Higgenbotham had been pounding on the door screeching that Claire had tried to poison her baby. The next thing she knew, two uniformed policemen had arrived to arrest her.

They'd actually been quite nice about it. Politely informing her that she'd have to come downtown with them before the taller one recited the Miranda rights to her. It still seemed like some kind of crazy nightmare.

But looking around the dismal holding room, she knew it was all too real.

The door opened and Mitch walked inside. Relief tightened her throat as she flew into his arms. "I'm so glad you're here."

"It's okay," he whispered against her hair, holding her tightly in his embrace.

She tilted her head back to look at him. "I tried to call you."

"My cell phone battery must be out again," he said, then muttered an oath under his breath as his gaze wandered around the cell.

Claire closed her eyes as he held her. Maybe A.J.

had found a way to contact him. Her roommate had been the next person she'd called. A.J. was in the middle of a court case but she had advised Claire over the telephone in her calm, reassuring way. *Don't worry and don't say anything. I'll be down there as soon as I can.*

"Tell me exactly what happened," Mitch said, gazing into her eyes.

She shook her head in disbelief. "I'm still trying to figure that out myself. Mrs. Higgenbotham accused me of poisoning Cleo and the next thing I knew, I was under arrest."

"Poisoning Cleo?" Confusion clouded his blue eyes. "That doesn't make sense."

"I know. All I did was give her some sausages from breakfast." Claire searched for some reasonable explanation. "Maybe they made her sick. I just don't understand how the police could arrest me for it."

"Is Cleo...alive?"

She nodded, remembering vividly how Cleo had humped against one of the cop's legs while he was arresting her. "She's very much alive. Acting very strangely though."

The door to the cell opened and a blond woman on crutches hobbled inside. She wore a plastic cop's badge clipped to the lapel of her jacket and held a thick file folder in one hand.

Mitch scowled at her. "Not now, Elaine."

Elaine? Why was Mitch was on a first name basis with a cop?

"Sorry, Mitch, but this can't wait any longer."

Elaine tossed the file onto the table, then fell heavily into the chair. "We need a statement from you, Miss Dellafield. Now we have the veterinarian's lab report right here, so there's no use telling us that you had nothing to do with the incident."

"Us?" Claire looked from Elaine to Mitch and back again. Something definitely wasn't right here. "I have no idea what you're talking about."

Elaine glanced up at Mitch. "Have you told her?"

"No," he said tightly.

Elaine sighed, then turned back to Claire. "We've been investigating Dick Vandalay for trafficking in illegal imported aphrodisiacs. One of which was found in the poodle's system."

Claire stared at the woman, trying to process everything at once. But only one word stuck out in her mind. "We?"

"Do you want to tell her or should I?" Elaine asked Mitch.

"Tell me what?" Claire exclaimed, her knees growing shaky.

Mitch stepped forward. "I think you'd better sit down, Claire."

A roaring sounded in her ears. "Just tell me."

His jaw clenched. "I've been working undercover as a bouncer at The Jungle for the last month. Searching for evidence to put away Vandalay."

She stared up at him, not wanting to believe it. Because if she did, everything else that had happened between them was a lie.

"It's only a matter of time until we bring Vandalay down," Elaine informed her, though she might as well have been conversing in Greek.

Claire couldn't comprehend a word the woman said. She kept staring at Mitch, waiting for him to tell her this was some kind of joke. A simple misunderstanding.

But nothing about Mitch seemed simple anymore.

As the silence stretched between them, she kept remembering all those little signs that pointed the way to the truth. How Mitch seemed much too intelligent to work at a dead-end job. How he'd accused Ramirez of ripping off restaurants. Even Albert had seen the truth, commenting that Mitch acted more like a cop than a bouncer.

Then she thought of last night, when she'd seen him standing over her computer. He'd swept away her questions with a night of passion. *Because he wanted to hide something?*

"Claire, let me explain," he began.

But she backed away from him, slowly shaking her head.

"There's a possibility you can cut a deal," Elaine informed her. "But that means full disclosure of all your business arrangements with Vandalay, your supply sources and the names of the couriers."

She took a deep breath, knowing there was more at stake here than her broken heart. She remembered A.J.'s advice on the phone. "I won't say a word until my lawyer is present."

Elaine shrugged, then grabbed her crutches and lifted herself out of the chair. She headed for the door, turning just as she reached it. "You coming, Mitch?"

He shook his head, then took a step closer to Claire. "Please understand. I was just doing my job."

His words cut her like a knife. She sucked in a deep breath of air, telling herself she could survive this. "Frankly, my dear, I don't give a damn."

MITCH STOOD OUTSIDE THE holding room, waiting impatiently while Claire conferred with one of her roommates. Attorney A. J. Potter didn't so much as glance at him when she'd passed him in the hallway over an hour ago.

He was glad Claire had a sharp lawyer in her corner. Considering the evidence against her, he was afraid she was going to need one.

Mitch closed his eyes, knowing as long as he lived, he'd never forget the look on Claire's face. The complete devastation. If only he could find a way to make her understand. To make her trust him again.

But she wouldn't even allow him inside the room with her.

The door to the holding room suddenly opened and Mitch pushed himself away from the wall, hoping to catch a glimpse of her. But A.J. prevented that by closing the door firmly behind her.

"Looks like you've arrested the wrong woman, Detective Malone."

"I didn't arrest her," Mitch said, though he'd done

much worse. He'd lied to her. At the same time he was making love to her.

"How is she?" he asked.

A.J. arched a brow. "She's just been arrested and discovered that the man she loves has been using her to gather information in a police investigation. How do you think she's doing?"

The man she loves. Mitch clung to those words, even as the rest cut him to ribbons. "We've got to fix this. I know she's innocent."

"Well, that makes two of us," A.J. said. "Now get a search warrant for the home of Albert Ramirez and maybe we can convince your partner and the rest of the police force that Claire's not to blame for whatever happened to Cleo."

He stared at her. "Ramirez?"

"Claire met him this morning at a diner on Thirty-second Street in midtown. He told her he wanted to finish the interview, but he had breakfast waiting for her when she got there. Eggs, hash browns, sausages."

His jaw tightened. "Are you saying he's the one who spiked those sausages?"

A.J. shrugged. "All I know is what Claire told me. Apparently, he was interested in a lot more than answering her questions. And quite upset when she didn't eat her breakfast."

Ramirez. Mitch's mind whirled as he considered the implications. Had he and Elaine been looking at the wrong man all along? They'd suspected Vandalay because of his criminal family connections. But Ramirez was a regular at The Jungle. And Mitch already knew the man was a thief. And a complete jerk.

"Damn," he muttered. "This is all my fault. I should have figured it out sooner."

"I agree," A.J. replied, not cutting him any slack. "Now what are you going to do about it?"

THREE HOURS LATER, CLAIRE looked up as the door to the holding room opened and A.J. walked inside.

"The cops found a stash of bootleg Viagra and other assorted illegal aphrodisiacs at the Ramirez place," she said without preamble. "And a waiter at the diner witnessed Ramirez sprinkling something on your plate before you showed up. So Albert Ramirez is now under arrest and you're free to go."

Claire nodded, feeling slightly numb. But beneath that numbness was a white hot anger that threatened to boil over given the least provocation.

"Mitch insists on talking to you," A.J. said, picking her briefcase off the floor. "If you'd rather avoid him, I know a back way out of this place."

Claire shook her head, ready to face him, before she lost the edge of her anger and completely fell apart. "Send him in."

16

CLAIRE STOOD UP, HER body tense as she waited for Mitch to walk through the door. She thought about the first day she'd met him in the back alley outside The Jungle. How his complete unawareness of her had stung her pride.

The skirt had changed all that. Mitch had kissed her the one and only time she wore it. Little did she know that his interest after that night had nothing to do with her and everything to do with his case.

Mitch was a cop.

She kept repeating those words over and over in her mind, trying to comprehend them. Every moment they'd spent together had been a lie. So why did she want to run into his arms when the door to the holding room opened and Mitch walked inside?

Claire stood her ground as Mitch looked at her warily.

"You okay?" he asked.

She gave a stiff nod. "What do you want?"

He took a step toward her. "I want to tell you that I never meant to hurt you. That what happened last night...wasn't part of this."

She closed her eyes for a moment, remembering the

way he'd made love to her. Then she remembered something he'd said last night. Something she'd considered a joke until just now. "You thought I put something in your food last night. An aphrodisiac. Is that the reason you made love to me? Did you feel coerced?"

"No," he exclaimed, his eyes dark with denial. "I wanted to make love to you. I still want you. More than anything."

She wanted so much to believe him. But she'd already let Mitch Malone fool her for much too long.

"Just tell me one thing," she said at last, her jaw aching. "Do they pay you overtime for working the night shift?"

His nostrils flared. "I know I deserve that. Just like I know you have no reason to trust me now."

"You were very good," she admitted, trying to distance herself from the pain. "All the little things you did to earn my trust. Like rescuing me from that mugger in Central Park. And those dinners with Mrs. Cudahy."

She looked up at him, suddenly curious. "Are they both cops, too? Was that all just part of your strategy to get closer to me? To gain my confidence?"

"No," he said tightly. "I never really believed you were involved. But I wasn't the only one calling the shots on this case. I had a job to do."

"So did I," she shot back. "Did it ever occur to you that your investigation could put an end to my research project? Maybe even to my career? There aren't too many professors with felony records working at universities."

"The charges were dropped," he replied.

"Thanks to A.J." She drew in a deep breath, struggling to remain calm. No matter what, she wouldn't let him see her cry.

"Claire," he entreated, moving closer to her. But she held up both hands to ward him off.

"You know what the worst part is?" she said softly. "I don't know who you really are. All the things you told me about your grandmother and your friends. The fun we had together. Was any of it real?"

He reached out and grasped her shoulders, as if he wanted to shake the truth into her. "It was all real, Claire. I love you."

She would have given anything to hear those words eight hours ago. Now they just dropped like stones in the empty place that used to hold her heart. When he saw her expression, he dropped his hands from her shoulders and took a step back.

"I talked to Dick Vandalay a few minutes ago," she said with a calmness that belied the turmoil inside of her. "He thinks I was helping you gather information on him and his customers. He ordered me never to step foot in The Jungle again. My research project is finished."

"Hell, Claire," he raked his hand through his hair. "Maybe if I talked to him..."

"Forget it," she said in a clipped tone. "I don't need or want your help."

"So now what?"

"Now I'll be going back to Indiana, to try to find some way to keep my job."

"What about us?" he asked, the bleakness in his blue eyes matching the tone of his voice. "Damn it, Claire! Don't throw this away because of one mistake. I know I screwed up. Big time. Just give me another chance."

She wanted to believe him. If only she could erase this day from her memory bank and pretend it never happened. But the pain went too deep. Pain she never wanted to experience again. If she let Mitch back into her heart, she might never survive the next time he broke it.

"Why?" she challenged. "You're not the marrying kind, remember? Besides, most of your relationships last less than a month, so we're right on schedule."

A muscle flexed in his jaw. "I've never experienced anything like this with any other woman."

"I know," she said wryly, her voice filled with bitterness. "This time you were just doing your job."

His Adam's apple bobbed in his throat. "I love you, Claire."

She couldn't do this anymore. Her resolve was beginning to crumble. She circled around him and headed blindly for the door. "Goodbye, Mitch."

"Claire," he called, bringing her to a stop right on the threshold.

She took a deep, steadying breath, but didn't turn around. "What?"

"I never meant to hurt you."

She gave a shaky nod, then left him and his lame apologies behind. She'd been living in some kind of dream world, imagining a life together with Mitch. But he belonged in this city. She belonged in Indiana.

Claire blinked back tears as she walked out of the police station, telling herself that Mitch had never made her any promises. Just the opposite, in fact. He'd taken their relationship one day at a time. One lie at a time.

But they'd been such beautiful lies.

MITCH SAT AT THE TABLE IN the holding room, his face buried in his hands. He wanted so much to run after her, to convince Claire that his love was real.

But why should she believe him?

Especially when proof of his deception was still in her computer. A.J. had promised to get rid of that damn diskette for him, though he knew she'd do it for Claire's sake rather than his own.

The door creaked open, and for a moment he let himself hope that she'd come back. But when he looked up he saw Elaine moving into the room on her crutches.

"Is she gone?" Elaine asked, dropping carefully into the chair opposite him.

He nodded, his throat too tight to speak.

"Hell, Mitch, I blew it," she said with a sigh.

He cleared his throat. "We both blew it."

Elaine shook her head. "You were never convinced

that Claire was involved in the case. But I had to keep pushing. I had to get vengeance on the man who I thought gave the order to push me down those stairs." Then tears suddenly filled her eyes. "Damn it, Mitch, why weren't you there for me?"

"I'm sorry," he said, the words sounding hollow to his ears. Would he always screw up with the women who mattered to him?

She shook head, hastily wiped her eyes. "I'm the one who's sorry. I never should have said that. And I never should have gone into that building alone. I wanted to prove that I could handle it on my own."

He knew how much Elaine feared she'd never work as an investigator again. "I should have been there for you."

"We both made mistakes," she admitted, the anger leaving her just as quickly as it had come. "My mistake was in blaming you. And pushing you too hard in this case. I'm the reason you lost Claire."

"I lost her all by myself," he said, reaching for her hands.

Elaine grasped them in her own. "Then go get her back."

"It's too late." He took a deep breath, ready to change the subject. "So how do we know for certain Vandalay isn't connected with Ramirez?"

Even as he asked the question, he knew that it didn't really matter. That he just wanted some justification for the weeks he'd spent lying to her. But he knew in his heart there was no excuse.

"Ramirez just made a full confession," Elaine told him. "He gave us the names of his couriers and his supplier. Vandalay is completely cleared."

He breathed a sigh of relief. "Good."

"Give her some time," Elaine said softly. "Maybe she'll come around."

But Mitch knew it was too late. Now he just had to figure out how he could possibly live the rest of his life without Claire in it.

THREE WEEKS LATER, CLAIRE sat at her computer desk, putting the finishing touches on her research project. After the study at The Jungle had tanked, she'd put off going back to Penleigh and instead focused all her attention on her aphrodisiac study. It had gone amazingly well, the words and ideas flowing faster than her fingers could type. It was a heady feeling and one that she'd never experienced before.

For the first time in her life, she felt like a real anthropologist.

Thanks to Kate Gannon, Claire had been able to contact all the former owners of the skirt and get their stories. Torrie, Chelsea McDaniels, and Gwen Fleming. Albert Ramirez had proved helpful, too, and her visits to his jail cell had enlightened her on the modern use and distribution of aphrodisiacs.

Through it all, she'd tried to push thoughts of Mitch completely out of her mind, but he still snuck in once in a while. Usually at night.

Finally satisfied with the report, she hit the save button, then settled back in her chair.

"Hope I'm not interrupting," chimed a voice from her doorway.

Claire turned to see Petra arrayed in a full-length gown of red sequins. "Wow. What's the occasion?"

"My gallery show opens next Friday." She spun in a slow circle. "Do you really like it?"

"It's fabulous," Claire replied, with a twinge of something oddly like envy. Petra had never held back from life. She always grabbed it with both hands and held on for the ride.

"You're coming, aren't you?" Petra asked.

"Of course." Claire clicked off the computer, needing a break. "I reminded A.J. and Sam, too, although they may already have plans."

"And I reminded Mitch," Petra said breezily.

Claire stiffened. "You did?"

"He has to be there," Petra exclaimed. "His sculpture is the highlight of the show. I can't wait to see how much it brings at the auction."

Petra had been so impressed with Mitch's physique in that loincloth that she'd erased the few parts resembling Delmore and even renamed the sculpture. Every time Claire entered Petra's apartment, she'd averted her gaze from "the Malone." Even though it was only a sculpture of his body from the neck down, it was enough to remind her of what she'd lost.

Petra had even gotten the proportions beneath the

loincloth right, although Claire had refused to divulge the information when asked.

"Did he...say if he's planning to come?" Claire inquired, trying to sound nonchalant.

"Nothing definite," Petra replied. "And not a word about you. I think he's deeply hurt."

"He's deeply hurt?" She gaped at her godmother in disbelief. "He's the one who lied, who used romance like a shovel to dig for information."

"But you're the one who's running away."

Claire stared at her dearest friend. So much for her godmother's threat to kill Mitch if he broke her heart. Instead, Petra was taking his side!

"Penleigh is my home," Claire said evenly, refusing to get drawn further into a futile argument. "Fortunately, I have enough confidence in the potential of this new study that I might just be able to keep it."

"Home is where the people you love are," Petra reached for her hand. "I'm going to tell you something that your father only wanted revealed in case of an emergency. I'm not quite sure this fits the definition, but I certainly consider it critically important. Because you're about to throw away something you may never get back again."

Claire had never seen Petra this serious before. Apprehension skittered up her spine. "What did my father tell you?"

Petra took a deep breath and Claire could feel the woman's fingers shaking in her hand. "Twenty-five years ago, Marcus came to New York City a young man, ready to take on the anthropology world. But what he didn't expect was to find love along the way. A woman who saw him as a man instead of a professor. A woman who inspired passion. A woman named Elizabeth."

Claire stared at her in disbelief. "So what happened?"

Petra's gaze softened on her. "Elizabeth had Marcus's baby. A beautiful girl."

A roaring sounded in Claire's ears. "Me?"

Petra nodded. "Only he was certain the love of his life could never fit into his world. And she was just as sure he'd never fit into hers. She wasn't prepared to raise a child on her own and planned to give you up for adoption. Until Marcus persuaded her that you would have a good life with him. That you would never want for anything."

Myriad thoughts whirled around in Claire's brain. *Why hadn't her father ever told her the truth?* "So my mother is...here? Living in New York City?"

Petra shook her head, compassion gleaming in her green eyes. "No. When your father told you she had died, it was the truth. Elizabeth was killed in a boating accident when you were just two years old."

"So why didn't he ever tell me he was my biological father?"

A shadow of a smile lit Petra's face. "Because your mother was one of the subjects in his research study at The Jungle."

Claire's heart fell to her toes. "That can't be true.

My father would never compromise his research that way."

"It is true."

"But I still have my adoption papers."

"They were real," Petra said. "Elizabeth refused to list his name on the birth certificate to protect him. You see, someone had already leaked the fact that Professor Marcus Dellafield was planning to adopt a baby girl. That was the reason his research study hit the major media outlets. People love that kind of sentimental spin to a story."

"But the truth would have ruined his professional reputation," Claire mused aloud. "Compromised his career."

Petra nodded. "That's the reason Elizabeth suggested a private adoption. Because what good would it have done the public to know about their love affair? On the other hand, his research study was having a positive effect. Penleigh was seeing both increased enrollments and donations. Other academics were looking seriously at dating habits that evolved from the sexual revolution."

Claire was still reeling from the bombshell Petra had just dropped in her lap. "Were they really in love?"

"It was a sight to behold," Petra said wistfully.

Claire sat in silence, waiting for a sense of betrayal to overtake her. But it didn't come. Marcus Dellafield had always been her real father, even before she knew they shared the same genes. He'd made a wonderful home for her and loved her unconditionally.

Perhaps her experience with Mitch had something to do with her empathy, too. She knew now that love could be just as messy as it was marvelous. As Marcus Dellafield had discovered when he'd come to New York City twenty-five years ago.

She looked up at Petra, her throat tight. "Why are you telling me all of this?"

"Because I want you to make your choices with your eyes wide open." She squeezed Claire's hands in her own. "Marcus could have stayed here. Even though Elizabeth hadn't made him any promises. He could have chosen her over his career. Love over security. He could have chosen a life of passion."

"And you're afraid I'm following in his footsteps?"

Petra didn't say anything for a long moment, then she reached out to cup Claire's cheek. "I'm afraid you'll want to play it safe for the rest of your life. And that's no way to live, Claire."

Then Petra got up and walked out of the room without another word.

Claire stared after her, a jumble of emotions stretching the limits of her heart. There was so much to risk. So much to lose. And absolutely no guarantees.

She knew she had a choice to make. She could hibernate in the relative security of Penleigh without ever putting her heart in jeopardy again.

Or she could pursue passion.

17

CLAIRE KNEW IF SHE wanted to get Mitch back, she needed to use every weapon in her arsenal. So the day of Petra's show at the Ledbetter Gallery, she prepared with meticulous care. Splurging on the full treatment at a spa, including a facial, manicure and pedicure. Visited a beauty salon that charged so much money for a shampoo and style that she briefly considered enrolling in cosmetology school. She even bought a new pair of shoes. There was only one thing missing.

The skirt.

At six fifty-five that evening, Claire paced back and forth across her living room at The Willoughby, waiting for A.J. to bring her the skirt. What were the chances that all three of them needed to wear it on the same day?

Sam had worn it this morning, then traded the real skirt for A.J.'s fake one this afternoon. A.J. had left around five, but promised to bring the skirt back to Claire before seven. Only she wasn't here yet.

Did Claire dare attend the gallery showing without it? Take the chance that she could win Mitch over all on her own?

Of course, he might not even be there—especially if

he had lost interest in her. He certainly hadn't bothered to call or stop by since that day at the police station. She hadn't seen or heard from him in three weeks. Not a word. And even though that's exactly what she'd told him she wanted, it still hurt. A little attention would have been nice. Candy. Flowers, even. In her opinion, groveling was a lost art form.

But that's what worried her. Maybe Mitch didn't feel the need to grovel. Maybe he'd already moved on to someone else.

She shoved that unwelcome thought out of her mind, then headed for her bedroom. With or without the skirt, she had to go to that gallery and find out for herself if Mitch wanted her back. Rifling through her closet, she found the skirt knockoff she'd bought at Bloomingdale's all those weeks ago. Pulling it on, Claire hoped Mitch would at least make a brief appearance at the Ledbetter Gallery.

It would be much easier to encounter him in a public setting than to track him down at his apartment. He might not even live there anymore. For all she knew, he'd used it as a cover while he had worked at The Jungle.

As she walked out into the hallway, the clock chimed seven times.

"Claire?"

She hurried into the living room to see A.J. unzipping the black skirt she wore. "You made it!"

"Sorry I'm late. The traffic is horrific." She stepped

out of the skirt, then handed it to Claire. "There's only one problem. I'm not sure this is the right skirt."

"What do you mean?"

"There were two skirts in my closet this morning—the real one and my knockoff. Sam wore what she thought was the real skirt, then traded with me this afternoon. But I think there was some kind of mixup. It sure didn't seem to work for me today."

Claire removed her own knockoff skirt to compare the two.

"Do they look the same to you?"

A.J. squinted at the two skirts. "It's too dark in here to tell. Let's go to Sam's room. It has the best light."

They both walked down the hallway to Sam's bedroom, then stood in front of the large window overlooking Central Park. A.J. held up one skirt to the light while Claire held up the other.

"What do you think?" A.J. asked, looking back and forth between them.

"That one seems to have more of a sheen to it," Claire replied, nodding toward the skirt in A.J.'s hand. If she stood here much longer, it wouldn't matter which skirt she wore. Mitch would be gone.

"I think you're right," A.J. agreed. "This one must be the real thing."

Claire tossed the skirt she held on Sam's bed, then A.J. handed her the other skirt. She stepped into it and zipped it up, hastily tucking in her blouse. "How do I look?"

"Nervous," A.J. replied honestly.

"I guess that's better than nauseous." Then Claire was out the door.

Fortunately, Mrs. Higgenbotham and Cleo weren't around to slow her down. She ran to the elevator, punching the button three times until it finally opened for her. Down in the foyer, Franco frowned as she raced out of the elevator.

"Everyone is in a hurry this evening," he said, blocking the door. "Rush, rush, rush."

"Please, Franco," she said, resisting the urge to push him out of the way. "I have to go. This could be the most important night of my life."

"I know," he replied. "Petra told me all about it." He placed his hand gently on her shoulders. "Now, I want you to take a deep breath."

She did as he asked, finding it actually did help her relax a little."

"That's better." He gave her shoulders a reassuring squeeze. "Now, no matter what happens tonight, there's something important I want you to remember."

"What?" she asked, sneaking a look at the clock on the wall. Seven-ten.

He smiled. "There's no place like home."

"There's no place like home," she echoed, wishing she could tap her heels together and be whisked off to the Ledbetter Gallery. But Franco found her a taxi almost immediately and she was on her way.

As she sat in the back seat, the taxi driving her to her destiny, she thought about what Franco had said.

She knew in her heart that her home was in this city now.

With the man that she loved.

Twenty minutes later, she stepped out of the cab in front of the Ledbetter Gallery. The same delicious power she'd felt at The Jungle the first night she'd worn the skirt washed over her. It must be the real one. She felt invincible. Beautiful. Alluring. As if no man could resist her.

But there was only one man who mattered.

Unfortunately, Mitch was nowhere in sight. She scanned the crowded gallery, her hopes crashing down when she realized he must not have come.

"You're here!" Petra flew over and embraced her. "You look lovely."

"So do you," Claire replied, determined not to put a damper on Petra's big night, despite her own disappointment.

"Isn't this a wonderful turnout?" Petra exclaimed, then she leaned closer to Claire and lowered her voice. "The mayor is here and the critic from *Art Today* magazine just raved about 'the Malone.' He wants the magazine to do a feature on me. Can you imagine?"

"I'm so happy for you," Claire said and meant it.

"Where's Mitch?" Petra asked, looking around the gallery.

Claire swallowed. "I don't think he's here."

"Well, I'm sure he will be soon." Petra reached for a glass of wine from a passing waiter. "Don't worry."

But Claire wasn't so certain. Mitch might want to avoid seeing her again. Maybe he didn't miss her at all.

"I'd better go mingle," Petra said, draining her wineglass in one gulp. "The auction is going to begin soon."

Claire walked around the gallery, admiring the works on display. Then she came upon "the Malone," showcased on a marble column in the center of the room and lit with an accent light.

If she couldn't have Mitch, maybe she could have this sculpture of him. The one momento of the most wonderful summer of her life.

There was only one problem. Thanks to the expense of living in New York City and her spree at the spa today, her bank account was almost barren. She knew Petra's work usually went for hundreds of dollars, sometimes thousands. So how could she possibly afford to buy "the Malone"?

Claire reached for her purse, counting the measly amount inside her billfold. Twenty-two dollars and seventeen cents. She pulled her hand out of her purse and her trapiche emerald ring flashed in the light.

She stared at it, knowing it had been appraised for more than three thousand dollars. In fact, the appraiser had been so impressed by the rare quality of the gem, he'd offered to buy it on the spot. The crack of a gavel hitting marble startled her out of her reverie.

The auction was about to begin.

MITCH STOOD IN A FAR corner of the gallery, sipping a glass of wine. How soon could he leave without looking rude? Petra was busy entertaining her circle of admirers, mostly young men. The other patrons were oohing and aahing over her work, a few throwing assessing glances at Mitch, thanks to the sculpture she'd named "the Malone".

He didn't see the resemblance, but he wasn't in the habit of staring at his body. And truthfully, it made him more than a little uncomfortable to have it on display for all the world to ogle.

There was only one woman he wanted ogling him and she was nowhere in sight. The only reason Mitch had come here tonight was to catch a glimpse of Claire. It had only been three weeks, but it felt like three decades. He'd picked up the phone a hundred times, but what could he say that hadn't already been said? She knew where to find him. And she obviously wasn't interested in looking.

When Petra had called to invite him to the showing, he'd been half hoping that it was another not-so-subtle matchmaking attempt. He would have even worn a leather loincloth if that's what Claire wanted. He'd do anything to prove his love to her.

Petra pounded a gavel against a slab of marble. "Attention, everyone. It's time for the auction."

She waited as the crowd gathered around her. "As most of you know, I've decided to sell 'the Malone' to the highest bidder and give the proceeds to charity. I hope you'll all be as generous with your pocketbooks as you are with the wine the gallery is providing to-night."

Soft laughter floated throughout the room.

Mitch moved back behind a decorative tree. Once the bidding got started, he'd make a quick exit. Maybe go home and indulge in a Humphrey Bogart marathon. Commiserate with another man about women.

Of all the gin joints in all the world, she had to walk into mine.

Then he looked up and saw her. Claire stood near Petra, looking so hot that he was surprised the floor didn't melt under her. She wore a jade silk blouse and a short black skirt. *The skirt?* Mitch didn't know or care. The only thing that mattered was the fact that she'd come here tonight.

He moved farther behind the tree, suddenly wary that if Claire spotted him, she'd disappear from his life again.

"Shall we start the bidding at five hundred dollars?" Petra asked.

"Five hundred," called out a portly gentleman standing near Claire. Mitch was amazed that the man could pay attention to the auction, much less bid, with her so close to him.

"I bid six hundred," chimed an elderly woman with an ebony cane.

"One thousand," came a voice from the back of the crowd.

The elderly woman tapped her cane on the floor. "Fifteen hundred."

The bids for "the Malone" quickly escalated, but Mitch only had eyes for Claire. He feasted on her, noting every curve, and every freckle. Remembering how perfect she'd felt in his arms. He'd been a fool to let her walk away from him once. He'd be damned if he let her do it again.

"We have a bid of three thousand dollars," Petra shouted over the room. "Going once. Going twice..."

"Three thousand, twenty-two dollars and seventeen cents," Claire called out in a clear, steady voice.

Mitch stood right behind her now and her bid inexplicably made his heart leap. Maybe he had a chance with her after all.

"Why spend that kind of money for a sculpture," Mitch asked, watching as she slowly turned around to face him, "when you can have the real thing?"

Petra gasped and the entire gallery fell silent.

Claire moistened her lips. "At what cost?"

He stepped toward her. "The body is free. The heart already belongs to you."

He heard several feminine sighs as every guest turned their attention to see Claire's response.

Her expression softened and he swore he saw love shining in her eyes. But maybe just the sight of her after so long was making him delusional. He felt the same dizzy rush he'd experienced the night they'd made love. A rush he wanted to feel all over again, every day for the rest of their lives. But he couldn't blame it on the skirt. It was all because of the woman who wore it.

"And what do I have to give in return?" she whispered.

Every head in the place turned to look at him. It was like the tennis match of love.

"Your heart. Your trust." He sucked in a deep breath. "Neither one of which I've earned. But I will. If you just give me enough time."

She stepped toward him and his breath caught in his throat. "How much time do you need?"

"Does fifty years sound reasonable?"

"How about seventy?" A smile teased her lips. "Studies show that men tend to be slow learners."

"Okay, seventy." He pulled her into his arms. "But only if I can conduct a research study of my own."

"What kind of study?" she asked, her lips parting as he lowered his head toward her.

"Human mating habits for two people who are crazy in love."

She circled her arms around his neck. "I volunteer to be your one and only subject.

"Professor, you've got a deal." Then he kissed her and didn't intend to stop for a very long time.

"What about 'the Malone'?" someone cried as Mitch and Claire lost themselves in each other's arms.

"I bid ten thousand dollars," Petra replied. "Going once, going twice. Gone."

She slammed the gavel down on the marble counter, unshed tears shining in her eyes. "It will make the perfect wedding gift."

____Epilogue____

CLAIRE, SAM AND A.J. stared at the three skirts laid out on the sofa. Their lease was up tomorrow and they'd decided to celebrate by introducing their boyfriends to one another. Sam's boyfriend, Josh, had already arrived and was opening a bottle of wine in the kitchen. Mitch had just called from his cell phone to tell Claire he was on his way up.

"The skirts all look identical to me," Sam said.

"I'm almost positive I wore the real one to Petra's show at the gallery," Claire insisted, then frowned down at the three skirts. I'm just not sure which one it is now."

The doorbell rang and Claire let Mitch inside. She greeted him with a light kiss, then made the introductions.

"You're just in time to help us figure out which skirt is the real one," Claire told him.

"What does it really matter?" A.J. asked. "We've all found our true loves. Let's just each take one."

"I'll tell you why it matters," Mitch said, as Josh returned from the kitchen with the wine. "Because I've already seen the effect that skirt has on men and I don't want my woman attracting every guy in the metropolitan area. Especially since she's about to become rich and famous."

Claire's heart tripped at the loving confidence Mitch had in her work. Thanks to Petra, her aphrodisiac study had been leaked to the New York media and was causing something of a sensation. She'd already fielded calls from some of the most prestigious universities in the country offering her a faculty position, as well as a publisher with a very appealing book offer.

"I second that," Josh replied, handing each of the women a glass of wine.

"Maybe we should each try on a skirt," Sam suggested, "and let the guys tell us which one is the real thing."

"That sounds simple enough," A.J. said. She swept up the skirts in her arms and headed down the hallway. "Let's go change."

"I'll be right back," Claire told Mitch, but he followed her into the hallway, grabbing her hand while the other two disappeared inside Sam's bedroom.

He gazed into her eyes. "I just want you to know right now that no skirt made me fall in love with you, Claire Dellafield. You did that all by yourself."

She circled her arms around his neck. "I did have *some* help, you know. Petra and Franco and Mrs. Higgenbotham and Cleo."

He grinned. "Does that mean we have to invite them to the wedding?"

"Not until we make it official."

"All right." He pulled a diamond ring from his shirt pocket. "Let's do it."

Claire's mouth fell open as he slid the vintage ring on her finger, but no words came out. The marquise diamond was exquisitely set on a platinum band. Claire's throat grew tight as she realized she'd made all the right choices. A man she loved. A career of her own making. A life that held so many wonderful promises.

"This was my grandmother's ring. She wanted me to give it to someone special."

She held out her hand, turning the ring so it caught the light. "It's absolutely beautiful."

"So are you." Then he pulled her into his arms for a long, deep kiss and Claire knew that of all the exotic places she'd been in the world, she'd never forget this apartment on the sixth floor of The Willoughby.

Sam stuck her head outside her bedroom door. "Claire, are you coming?"

She smiled up at Mitch. "I have to go put on a skirt. "Wait for me?"

"Forever."

* * * * *

No man can resist the skirt, even the most unlikely ones, A.J. discovers to her delight. Don't miss seeing the last single find her match in

SHORT, SWEET AND SEXY

by Cara Summers, available next month.

**Receive 2 FREE Trade books with 4 proofs
of purchase from Harlequin Temptation® books.**

You will receive:

Dangerous Desires: Three complete novels by
Jayne Ann Krentz, Barbara Delinsky and Anne Stuart

and

Legacies of Love: Three complete novels by
Jayne Ann Krentz, Stella Cameron and Heather Graham

**Simply complete the order form and mail to:
"Temptation 2 Free Trades Offer"**

<u>In U.S.A.</u>
P.O. Box 9057
3010 Walden Avenue
Buffalo, NY 14269-9057

<u>In CANADA</u>
P.O. Box 622
Fort Erie, Ontario
L2A 5X3

YES! Please send me *Dangerous Desires* and *Legacies of Love*, without
cost or obligation except shipping and handling. Enclosed are 4 proofs
of purchase from September or October 2002 Harlequin Temptation
books and $3.75 shipping and handling fees. New York State residents
must add applicable sales tax to shipping and handling charge.
Canadian residents must add 7% GST to shipping and handling charge.

Name (PLEASE PRINT)

Address   Apt. #

City   State/Prov.   Zip/Postal Code

TEMPTATION 2 FREE TRADES OFFER TERMS
To receive your FREE trade books, please complete the above
form. Mail it to us with 4 proofs of purchase, one of which can
be found in the lower right-hand corner of this page. Requests
must be received no later than November 30, 2002. Please
include $3.75 for shipping and handling fees and applicable
taxes as stated above. The 2 FREE Trade books are valued at
$12.95 U.S./$14.95 CAN. each. All orders are subject to
approval. Terms and prices are subject to change without
notice. **Please allow 6-8 weeks for delivery. Offer good in
Canada and the U.S. only. Offer good while quantities last.
Offer limited to one per household.**

HTPOPFT

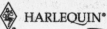

COOPER'S CORNER

The latest continuity from Harlequin
Books continues in October 2002 with

STRANGERS WHEN WE MEET
by Marisa Carroll

Check-in: Radio talk-show host Emma Hart thought Twin
Oaks was supposed to be a friendly inn, but fellow guest
Blake Weston sure was grumpy!

Checkout: When both Emma and Blake find their fiancés
cheating on them, they find themselves turning to one
another for support—and comforting hugs quickly turn to
passionate embraces....

HARLEQUIN®
Makes any time special ®

Visit us at www.cooperscorner.com

CC-CNM3

If you enjoyed what you just read,
then we've got an offer you can't resist!

Take 2 bestselling love stories FREE!

Plus get a FREE surprise gift!

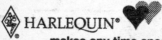

Princes...Princesses...
London Castles...New York Mansions...
To live the life of a royal!

In 2002, Harlequin Books lets you escape to a world of royalty with these royally themed titles:

Temptation:
January 2002—*A Prince of a Guy* (#861)
February 2002—*A Noble Pursuit* (#865)

American Romance:
The Carradignes: American Royalty (Editorially linked series)
March 2002—*The Improperly Pregnant Princess* (#913)
April 2002—*The Unlawfully Wedded Princess* (#917)
May 2002—*The Simply Scandalous Princess* (#921)
November 2002—*The Inconveniently Engaged Prince* (#945)

Intrigue:
The Carradignes: A Royal Mystery (Editorially linked series)
June 2002—*The Duke's Covert Mission* (#666)

Chicago Confidential
September 2002—*Prince Under Cover* (#678)

The Crown Affair
October 2002—*Royal Target* (#682)
November 2002—*Royal Ransom* (#686)
December 2002—*Royal Pursuit* (#690)

Harlequin Romance:
June 2002—*His Majesty's Marriage* (#3703)
July 2002—*The Prince's Proposal* (#3709)

Harlequin Presents:
August 2002—*Society Weddings* (#2268)
September 2002—*The Prince's Pleasure* (#2274)

Duets:
September 2002—*Once Upon a Tiara/Henry Ever After* (#83)
October 2002—*Natalia's Story/Andrea's Story* (#85)

Celebrate a year of royalty with Harlequin Books!

Available at your favorite retail outlet.

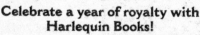

HARLEQUIN®
Makes any time special®

HSROY02